SOMETHING TOLD ME

TAKE CARE and ALOHA

11-05

SOMETHING TOLD ME
Against All Odds

Volume I

Wai Kiki

Copyright © 2005 by Wonder Horse Publishing
www.wonderhorsepublishing.com
e-mail info@wonderhorsepublishing.com

All Rights Reserved
No part of this book may be reproduced or transmitted in any form by any means, electronic or mechanical, including photocopying and recording, or by any information storage or retrieval system, without permission in writing from the copyright holder. Code Label: 042550

Printed in the United States of America
Honolulu, Hawaii

ISBN 0-9766647-2-0

Contents

INTRODUCTION xiii

CHAPTER ONE 1
Small Kid

CHAPTER TWO 7
Last One Out

CHAPTER THREE 17
Hot Situations

CHAPTER FOUR 25
Death Trap

CHAPTER FIVE 33
One Gutsy Move

CHAPTER SIX 55
Selective Hearing

CHAPTER SEVEN 63
Rapid Reaction

CHAPTER EIGHT 71
Surprise in the Dark

CHAPTER NINE 81
A Near Fatal Mistake

CHAPTER TEN   87
Warned But Helpless

CHAPTER ELEVEN   91
A Picnic Tragedy

CHAPTER TWELVE   99
Thank God for Traffic

CHAPTER THIRTEEN   107
A Sixty Secong Warning

CHAPTER FOURTEEN   113
Fire Trap Hotel

CHAPTER FIFTEEN   119
Don't Ask Questions

CHAPTER SIXTEEN   125
Point Blank

CHAPTER SEVENTEEN   137
Speed Sailing

CHAPTER EIGHTEEN   151
Trust In Faith

CHAPTER NINETEEN   171
Final Approach

ENDORSEMENTS   181

For Pat Lopes
Co-Director of Teachers Education
College of Education, University of Hawaii at Manoa

Her knowledge, expertise, patience and wonderful heart went beyond the call, to help me through this project.

ACKNOWLEDGEMENT AND MAHALO

Two people I must first acknowledge, my two friends, Pastor Moses Kaina and Pastor Luigi Figueroa, whose efforts planted the seed for me to write this book and speak about the miracles that I witnessed. They realized that I had stories to tell, to help other people strengthen their lives by demonstrating how the Lord has and still does work in my life. They constantly asked me over a two year period to write these stories into a book and share them with their congregations, but I declined their request, because I had no idea how to do a book. Well, I believe my friends called on their Big Boss upstairs to rattle my cage and wake me up.

On September 11, 1992, God gave me a major wake up call. Due to the nature of my work, I had to take my pilot boat and go out to sea to deal with Hurricane Iniki, a "Category 4" storm that was slamming into Hawaii. At the height of the storm, something went wrong. I should have been the first fatality of Hurricane Iniki, but my life was spared because of a miracle. God gave me a last chance warning and I started writing the stories for my book that stormy day. This story I will share in the second volume of Something Told Me.

Having no clue about writing or computers, I luckily could depend on friends to help me with this major undertaking. Friends and family generously shared their knowledge, expertise and never ending patience in guiding me through each step of writing my stories and creating my book. Some friends taught me how to find my way around this high-tech computer world. Other people helped me to use proper grammar and forget the pidgeon English.

I continuously received support from other friends, as if this project had its own "plans" to be completed. The one common bond everyone shared is they believed in the message in this book and they believed I could do it. This further inspired me and I gained the confidence I needed as things began to fall into place. I didn't do this alone and I am grateful and thankful for everyone's help, and I finished most of it in the first two years.

Then, I put this project on the back burner, on a slow simmer for ten years. Every so often I would open it up, stir it a little, change this and add that and put it back to simmer again. As time went on I got brave and decided to publish this book myself. I admit, this made the book take a little longer to get done, I had to learn everything about self-publishing, so I attended seminars and did my homework just to make sure that being a publisher was something I could handle. It was the right choice.

One person who stayed close to this project for six years is my editor, a close friend and neighbor, Pat Lopes, Co-Director of Teacher Education at the University of Hawaii for twenty years. A professional in the field of education, I let her run this project, because of my crazy and busy schedule shuffling four professions at the same time. She nurtured this book along by doing whatever it needed and controlled everything to keep this project on track. With her constant support and patience, this book finally became a reality. It is only right that I dedicate this book to Pat Lopes.

I need to also acknowledge Pat's husband, and my friend, Danny Lopes, a talented songwriter and musician who wrote Hawaii's hit song, "A Part of Me, A Part of You." It was Danny who read this book years ago and took it home to show it to his wife. His total understanding and belief in this book allowed his wife to work with me for six years in order to see this project to completion.

When the publishing part of this effort finally came

into the picture, I needed to have someone produce and layout the manuscript and get it ready for the printers. My long time friend, Jackie Burke, took on the task to make it happen. She produces her own newspaper and amazes me with her knowledge of the computer graphics and the printing business.

Another good friend, Mark Brown, a noted art instructor and talented artist in Hawaii, did the cover art. He was able to take my idea of the first light of the sun peaking through a stormy sky and angry ocean and transferring it to canvas. The title of the painting is, "First light after the Hurricane."

The list of names of people that helped me over the past thirteen years on this project is long. I am forever grateful for all their help and will always appreciate their friendship and the talent that they brought to this project and book, "Something Told Me."

With Aloha, Wonder Horse Publications

INTRODUCTION

You are not a policeman and someone is about to be murdered right in front of you. You have no weapon, no way to call for help and you might be out-numbered. Would you risk your life to save that person? What if you saw someone drowning in a ferocious stormy ocean with 20 foot seas. You are not a rescue swimmer. Would you risk your life to save this person? *Something Told Me I could do it, and I did.*

In your lifetime, how often have you encountered a miracle in a precarious situation? Many people have close encounters of the "Angelic kind" once in a while, but in my life it happens over and over. These stories cover riveting true-life experiences of one person where a Miracle at the right time saved a deadly situation from turning fatal for many others and myself. Miracles and special blessings are experienced by millions of people around the world, but why me and why so often?

This book is not about religion. I am no authority on the subject and I did not grow up in a religious environment so you won't find anything religious in here. Instead you might think these stories are out of a movie like the "Adventures of Indiana Jones," but it's the real deal. It's action packed, exciting, educational and all true.

The stories in **Something Told Me** find me constantly in the middle of extraordinary events. After 40 years of dismissing these events as mere coincidence, it was time to testify that the will of God was responsible for my presence in these situations. I'm not a fireman, policeman or lifeguard, but born with a definite gift, I confront danger with total confidence to save someone's life. In many other situations, I found myself facing certain death, only to be saved by a miracle before time ran out. These stories vary in many different situations, locations and difficulties.

The title of this book is well founded. Throughout my life, and only during times of danger, an omnipotent *Voice* would address me. In each incident, it forewarned me of an upcoming situation. This premonition could be a few weeks or months in advance, or it might come within hours, minutes or seconds of the impending danger. This distinct *Voice* of contradictions is sometimes overwhelmingly strong yet silent, aggressive but calming; yet it guides me with a reassuring tone. Sometimes it is quickly heard and then gone, or it does not cease until I am actively involved in the situation at hand.

Where does it come from and what is it? How did I learn to listen more carefully to it? How did I condition myself to freely respond to it, rather than question it? A recurring theme throughout this book is total confidence, giving me the courage and calmness to react in different situations of danger. I learned that through God, protective Angels work together to provide me with no fear of the circumstances when all odds are stacked against me. With a strong trust in faith, I moved forward with no hesitation or fear because although I'm not a religious person, I do believe in God and Jesus Christ.

I was born with this special gift but didn't recognize it until later in life. During my days as a youth growing up in Hawaii, strangers often told me of an "aura" surrounding me, a presence of Angels blessing me. I didn't know how to respond and I wondered what they were talking about and wanted to ask them to explain what they just said, but they would mysteriously disappear. As time went on miraculous incidents continued to happen. I knew it was a gift of some sort but I didn't know what to say or do about this special blessing. I often wondered if it was my Hawaiian blood and the fact that I was raised in Hawaii. I had questions but no answers so I kept quiet about this.

Following four decades of holding on to a secret that something special was happening to me, I finally started telling stories of my experiences to close friends and family. The recurring events in my life could no longer be ignored and it soon became evident that all of this had to be written down and talked about. Friends and Pastors from different churches encouraged me to speak and write about my experiences and that ever-present voice was telling me the same thing:

" Glorify God. Write about your blessings.
"Speak to others about the miracles that you have known."

For many years I dismissed any thoughts of writing or speaking knowing it would be a major challenge for me because I was neither a writer nor a public speaker. This was way out of my realm. With family and friends to help me, I set out to teach myself everything I needed to know to get this book going. I couldn't type and I didn't know how to turn on a computer, let alone try to find my way through all this hi-tech computer jazz. Now, add to the fire my regular schedule of juggling four professions and multi-tasking projects, this book finally made it from the back burner, on a very slow simmer, to a final product in thirteen years.

I chose a handful of stories to write about out of a possible 300 or more incidents that I've been involved in. We divided these stories into three volumes and felt that what is written is enough to get this message across that miracles can happen because you have the same gift too. You just have to LISTEN, and have faith. If you believe in Miracles then no explanation is necessary. If you don't believe, then no explanation is possible.

Hello my new friend, welcome to my world. We're going on an adventure so have fun!

CHAPTER 1

Kailua stream as it is today with the sandbar blocking the ocean

SMALL KID TIME

Getting to know this Voice and being able to trust it and react to its calling wasn't something that happened overnight. I've been told that the gift of discernment is one of the many blessings I was born with. This meant I could pick out the right voice to hear and react to its message. This plan for me began to evolve soon after my birth. At a very young age, things were starting to happen.

My parents told me about an incident that happened to me when I was four or five years old that scared everyone. It was a family gathering of kids and adults down at a stream next to Kailua Beach for a day of fun, sun, food and games. Everyone was playing in the stream just ocean-side from where Buzz's Steak House sits today. Back then in 1955, the stream from Enchanted Lakes flowed freely into the ocean. Today a sand bar blocks the stream so the water can't flow into Kailua Bay.

According to Mom and Pop everyone got out of the water because it was time to eat lunch. A few minutes went by when they noticed I was missing and they started looking for me. In a few moments a horrifying sight caught their attention. I was still in the water but trapped by a large shark that came from the ocean and made its way into the shallow waters of the stream.

They saw the shark carving circles around me for a long time as I stood there very calmly. This monster was not making any effort to attack or carry me off to the deep blue sea. It was like an invisible fence formed by Angels suddenly appeared and protected me from this huge predator. Mom said I was trying to reach out and touch the shark, maybe to ride it. My Pops was the big hero because he jumped into the stream to take on the shark but it quickly left the area and went back out to Kailua Bay.

Years later my parents told me something about sharks that I would need to remember. People from Hawaii have certain Guardian Figures that belong to each family, kind of like a protector. It's called an Aumakua, a spirit that is good to you and protects you IF you return the respect it deserves. Our family's Aumakua is the shark. Some families have the turtle while others may have dolphins, whales, owls and other animals. My father was an avid diver, a lay-net fisherman and built his own fishing boats. The ocean was his life. I was seven when he told me something I never forgot.

"Our Aumakua is the shark. You are a shark. Respect them and they will never harm you."

Little did I know that twenty years later I would find myself in a serious situation with sharks and I would have to put all my trust in that statement just to survive.

Diamond Head as it looked back in the 1960's in my childhood.

Memories of my childhood are wonderful. I feel very fortunate to have been born and raised in Hawaii, the best place in the world to call home. I grew up in a nice middle class neighborhood on the slopes of Diamond Head, next to the Fort Ruger Army National Guard Base overlooking Waikiki. Dad was working at Pearl Harbor Naval shipyard and Mom was a housewife who sold Avon products on the side. She was very active in the Mormon Church and Dad was a part-time Catholic.

I have a twin sister who is totally opposite and different from me. She did basic girl stuff with Mom while I was a high adventure type kid and a rascal that thrived on mischief and adventure. Mom wanted to trade me in, and Dad often gave me the royal slap. I had the gift to design and build things at a very young age. This talent came from my Dad who was a jack of all trades. My artistic skills were already showing.

When I was a young lad my Mom would take my sister and me to church as often as possible, thinking God and all his Angels could help her rascal little boy. The neat thing I liked about our church was its location on the beach at Kahala. Every Sunday, at the beginning of church services, the adults would bow their heads and close their eyes for prayer. That's when my little friends and I would run out of church and head for the beach. At that time, church, God, miracles and Angels were of no concern for me. I was a kid who wanted to venture out on my bicycle with wings and explore the world. It was apparent in my young life that I would be an adventurer and a risk taker.

As I was growing up one of my talents started to take shape. One day my first grade teacher had the class draw a tree and everybody's tree looked like a lollipop. My picture of a tree was different. I was able to draw and copy a banyan tree outside our classroom, complete with its individual branches, roots on the ground and the picnic bench that sat under the tree, all layered in different shades of shadowing. The teacher screamed when she saw the picture and days later had a meeting with my Mom because she saw I was a gifted artist and maybe I should be sent to an art academy. By the time I reached grades four, five and six my art skills had escalated. Two other students and I were allowed to design murals of whatever holiday season it was, onto large blackboards using colored chalk. So at Easter time we had bunny rabbits, baskets and flowers all over the blackboards. At Halloween, Thanksgiving, Christmas and New Years we came up with festive and fun designs.

When I was eight years old I would be faced with my first serious situation. The life of another person depended on my actions. Will I be able to save this person or will I be too scared, turn away, and let this person die. Grab your fins and follow me if you dare to because we're in for a frightening experience.

CHAPTER 2

Ala Moana Beach Park, located near the shores of beautiful downtown Honolulu, across of Ala Moana Shopping Center.

LAST ONE

Last One Out happened at Ala Moana Beach Park. It was a typical gathering of family and friends but this particular picnic would be better for me because my Mom wouldn't be coming along, which meant this eight-year old rascal kid could act up and get into mischief. But today would be different for me. I would be the link between life and death for another and at the same time, experience the first shock of my young life.

The day started wonderfully, with the adults sitting around "talking story" and cooking. The teenagers played volleyball, while us younger kids went to swim near the shoreline. What a fun day for all involved! The weather was gorgeous, as usual, with the Pacific Ocean casting blue and silver tones against the horizon, while puffy white clouds paraded above us. The sky was tinted with orange and yellow hues; an indication of another beautiful sunset soon to come.

Ala Moana Beach Park, located near the shores of beautiful downtown Honolulu, is bordered by a long sandy beach and a reef that provides a barrier from unwanted creatures that may try to enter the swimming area.

Late in the afternoon, when it was almost time to go home, the grownups were cleaning our picnic area and calling the youngsters to come out of the water. I intended to be the last one out even though the air had become cooler and I had goose bumps all over my shivering body. I ignored the calls from the shore, and instead, chose to dive under the water again, this time moving further out into a deeper area. Soon I was the only one in the water, as the other kids finally decided to head in.

The water was six feet deep, and I was about thirty feet from the shore. I thought if I took a really deep breath, I might be able to swim underwater all the way to shore. I was barely a swimmer but I was going to try it today. This would be my first attempt at a long underwater swim. Treading water and sticking my head below the surface to blow bubbles was my big talent, and paddling like a dog was my way of propelling around. Being almost four feet tall, I felt okay about swimming alone.

So with all of these impressive credentials and with Mom not there, and believing that I was an expert swimmer, I inhaled a mouthful of air and dove down, thinking that the shoreline would be easy to find. The distance would be a great challenge for me. Could I make it? Visibility was limited, in fact, kind of murky. With my eyes wide open, I set my course and headed for shore. While swimming through the hazy waters, my senses got totally turned around and I ended up going into a deeper area.

When I surfaced, a frightening shock came over me because I had gone much further out and way beyond my limits. Everything my parents taught me about swimming with a buddy and not wandering off too far suddenly came to mind. I remembered their warnings, "Watch out for currents and undertows that can sweep you away and pull you under." The thought of danger entered my mind, as well as the crazy thought of something lurking in the waters around me.

Fortunately, I remained calm and didn't get scared, although I was a little concerned because a current was moving me very slowly out. Now I was far from shore and in deeper water. My plan was still the same. I was determined to swim underwater for as long as possible and head for shore. Taking a deep breath, I went down and down and down. I wasn't making much headway because I had never encountered a current before. I knew trouble surrounded me.

Persistence kept me going, but the lack of air told me it was time to come up. Just as I was about to surface, something caught my eye. Through all the distorted and murky surroundings I saw something below me. Almost completely out of air but with curiosity pushing me on, I dove a little deeper to see what it was. Propelling myself closer to this shadowy form brought me face to face with a horrifying sight. The shadow below me was a human figure. It was the body of Fred who was part of our group. Nothing could have prepared me for what I saw. Shock caused me to lose focus and I let out a deadly scream. Water rushed into my mouth instantly as I desperately went up for air.

When I reached the surface, choking and coughing overcame me. I thought I was going to drown. I swallowed too much water while gasping for air and I was not able to touch bottom. This situation was going to be fatal for me soon. If this was a bad nightmare, I was ready to wake up right now. I was in a near panic situation when an instant calmness came over me. All of a sudden, I was able to catch a good long breath of air. I started to scream and tried to attract someone's attention on shore. It didn't happen. The more I tried to scream, nothing happened. No sound came out of my mouth. After many attempts, my screams finally worked. Now I was screaming bloody murder and somebody heard. Eventually other people turned to see what was going on.

I was crying. Shock had set in. I was shaking from the discovery I had just made. When people heard my screams, I started to swim in, to tell them what I had just found. Then a Voice spoke softly to me. Something told me, "Go back." As if forced by a command, I did what no other youngster would have done. I went back to that same spot and with adrenaline pumping in me, dove down to get his body.

I searched all around and saw nothing. The water was very hazy and visibility was limited. Fred was gone and his body must have been moving away with the current. I shot back up for more air and went right back down again. On my next attempt, I changed course and saw a dark shadow before me. Something was telling me, "Do not be scared. Stay calm."

Was I ready for this horrible sight? As I got closer, the thought of seeing his lifeless body scared me. Fred's big eyes stared up at me, his lips and face were purple and swollen, and his gaping mouth was filled with foam. With a strength that came from an unknown source, I was able to grasp hold of him and swim to the surface. Slowly I kicked my feet into action and headed to shore. His head was next to mine and those dark eyes stared at me while the foam from his mouth spilled over my shoulders. His body color began to change to dark purple.

Dizziness and exhaustion caused me to let go and I left his body floating among the group of kids and adults gathered at the waters edge. Out of breath, I found myself falling onto the sand with no care about the commotion swirling around me. Only once did I glance in his direction. Foam continued to spew from his lips with gurgling sounds. I couldn't look again because I was scared and frightened beyond explanation. This was too much for an eight-year old to witness, because I was still a baby. In the meantime, a lifeguard and some of the adults were trying everything they could to save him. Things looked pretty bad for him. His limp body lay on the sand as we waited for the ambulance to arrive. I was in shock and sat there trying to make sense of everything. What if I hadn't stayed in the water? What if I hadn't decided to dive under again? How come no one knew he was missing? How long had he been down there? Would he die?

The ambulance finally arrived and he was rushed to Kaiser Hospital a half mile away. The sun had already set and the mood of the group was grim as they packed up to go home. There was nothing left to do but pray for him and his family. In the evening, a lady who was at the picnic called my Mom and told her what happened. She asked that a prayer circle be expanded and encouraged everyone to continue to pray for Fred's recovery. We knew his condition was critical. Only God could save him. It was a few days later when we found out he would be okay. The news was good and the doctors were able to save his life. The power of prayer worked, thanks to a miracle from God.

With all the excitement and commotion caused from the moment I brought his body to shore, his family never knew who found him on the ocean floor. As the years went on, our paths never crossed again. He lives in the Islands and I occasionally see him in a crowd or while in traffic maybe once a year. We've never had an opportunity to talk and I've often wondered if he knew about me, and his close brush with death.

When I was twenty-five, I met up with Fred's older brother Sol, and we've had a long lasting friendship for over twenty-years. I never mentioned anything to Sol about me finding his younger brother and saving his life. I always felt the subject was closed and should be left alone and I never told anyone about this incident back in 1958.

Well, when we at Wonder Horse Publications decided

to reveal this story, it was obvious to us that we would have to find this guy, Fred. So one evening, I called Sol and told him I had a book project that I was working on, and asked if he could read a story and let me know his thoughts. We met, had some small talk and I handed him some papers and never mentioned what the papers were about. I left thinking it would be days before I heard from him again. A few hours later, around midnight, I got a phone call from Sol. He was surprised and happy with what he just read because he had no idea I was connected with his younger brother's incident years ago. He asked me why I never told him about this before. I said it was part of my quiet nature. I didn't want to wave my own flag. It's not my style, so I kept quiet and never told anyone about it.

With Sol making the arrangements and giving Fred a heads up about me, I was finally going to meet him, 47 years later. On the day we drove out to see Fred, Sol briefed me on the condition of his younger brother. Turns out that Fred, who is now 55, suffered a stroke a few years earlier and his physical condition is limited. He is still sharp mentally and quick to crack a joke and he is living at a caregiver's home about 20 minutes outside of Honolulu.

When we finally met, we hugged and he greeted us with a joke and we all laughed. The first thing I said to him was, "Hey, have you been to the beach lately?" We talked about the incident that happened when we were both young kids and he remembered everything that took place that day until he started to drift into deeper water. He remembers what happened when he was dead and looking down at his body while he was being attended to on the beach and in the hospital and he also mentioned about the large amount of seawater and sand that was pumped out of his body.

Somehow, the many blessings from the powers that

be were preparing me at this young age to be a link with something of the supernatural. From this point on, I would find myself confronted with situations that would require my strength and wisdom to be able to survive a deadly confrontation for me or for someone else. At my young age I had no idea where life's road would lead me. After this incident, I pretty much forgot about it and went on being a typical rascal hanging with the boys. But now, that was the problem; hanging with the boys got us into some serious predicaments.

MAHALO and ALOHA

This letter confirms the story "Last One Out," in this book "Something Told Me". To respect his privacy, Fred's real name is not mentioned in the story. I am writing this letter on the behalf of my family and Fred to verify that this incident did take place in the summer of 1958, during a church picnic at Ala Moana Beach Park. Here are Fred's recollection of this near drowning incident:

He was 9 years old and remembers having fun and swimming with the other kids when he ventured out to far towards the notorious "Drop-Off" area where it gets deeper and suddenly, he went under. He sensed a deep fear while struggling for his life but never came back up and blacked out under water. Fred has no recollection of what happened while his body was on the ocean floor.

The next thing Fred recalls is rising far above and slowly drifting away from his body as it was laying on the beach with people crowding around him and the lifeguard was performing CPR. He looked up and noticed he was drifting towards an intense bright light, but felt it was not his time to die.

Suddenly he felt himself falling through a long bright tube back down towards earth and into his lifeless body. (CPR was successful.) Seeing the crowd of people standing over him, he noticed his face and body covered with sand as he coughed, spitting out sand, foam and ocean water he had swallowed. Fred recalls being placed into an ambulance and driving off to Kaiser Hospital and then blacked out again from secondary fear and pure exhaustion. His next recollection is opening his eyes, and as a frightened child, seeing strangers hovering over him (emergency room doctors and nurses) asking him questions and telling him he'll be okay.

Neither Fred nor I realized, until you told us through your story, that it was you who, as a young boy, had the persistence and tenacity to be the "Last One Out." While taking your last dive underwater, you discovered Fred on the ocean bottom, pulled his lifeless body to the surface and struggled to get him to shore while calling for help.

On the behalf of our family, Fred and I, we thank you.
Me Ke Aloha Pumehana. Mahalo a nui loa `ia `oe, Kiilehua.
Aloha Te Atua,

Dr. Solomon D.K. Nalua'I, M.D., D.D. (Ret.)

CHAPTER 3

HOT SITUATIONS
DIAMOND HEAD

I had an appetite for excitement at a very young age. I was probably eight when I carried my bicycle up to our roof, strapped myself into the parachute I made out of sheets, and rolled off the top of the roof. I crashed and burned many times. Next, I made wings and tied them to the handlebars of my bicycle. Thinking that I would be able to fly, I again rolled off the roof. Instead, I landed in my Dad's favorite Hibiscus plants destroying his prize flowers. That flight got me three slaps!

Then we had a crazy idea. What if we made a kite big enough to hang onto? After a few painful crashes, my friends and I perfected a giant kite that was fixed to a bicycle. A very steep hill in the neighborhood was our testing ground and I was the test pilot. We strapped some home made rockets onto the bike frame for that extra kick and I roared down the hill, experienced a short lift off and crashed into a parked car. We were happy knowing that our plan could turn into something fun. We had no idea that the sport of hang-gliding from a kite would become popular twenty years later.

My group of friends were way too advanced for our young age. We could invent and create anything. We were rocket scientists and bomb junkies. We had a few rules in our gang of misfits. No swearing, no stealing, no cigarettes, and no girls. Full of the "rascal adventuring spirit" and with no fear, we were forever pushing our limits in the pursuit of hot, daring and deadly games. It was obvious all of us were high-risk takers.

By the fourth grade, at the age of nine, my little band of friends and I were sneaking out of our bedroom windows at three in the morning to go joy riding on our bicycles down the hill into Waikiki. We would be back home before our parents got up to go to work. Our playground was inside and on top of Diamond Head Crater, which at that time was totally off limits to every one, except us kids. Back then one of our many camps was high atop Diamond Head, at the 700-foot level, in an old five-story bunker that overlooks Waikiki. Today, it's a popular tourist attraction with a great view of Honolulu.

When we were eleven, a friend got us into a hot situation. He was working on an invention we concocted from a couple of highly flammable cans of spray paint, the nozzle from a fire extinguisher and a can of lighter fluid and some matches, all connected together to make a flame thrower. We were in our secret clubhouse, in the basement of an old abandoned barracks at the Army base, when our little experiment exploded and instantly started an inferno that had the three of us trapped. The fire was intense as the flames spread quickly. We had no way of getting out of this death trap. Something Told Me, "Run down the hallway, you'll find a way out." Instantly calmness surrounded me and I was able to respond. After running down the dark hallway and finding an opening, I turned around to find my friends were not with me, so I ran back to get them. Their screams led me to a closet where they were huddled. Flames and dense smoke filled the area. The floor above us came down seconds after we ran for our lives.

A miracle happened at the right time to save our sorry butts because we were able to squeeze between a beam and a narrow opening to safety. We were lucky because we hid from the military police and the fire department. The fire was put out, saving most of the structure that was soon to be demolished anyway. We would have died under that building had I not listened to the voice that guided us to safety. Not so lucky was our friend who took the explosion point blank in his face and chest. He was a mess and we rushed him to the hospital in our neighborhood. Another friend's aunty was a nurse there and helped him to get better. God had his hands full watching over us!

Daring Danger

The intermediate school we attended was located on the opposite side of the Army base from where we lived. Our path to and from school every day was always more exciting and faster when we squeezed between fences to sneak through the base. Going around the base was a longer route, and included a very steep hill. When we got to the seventh grade, things changed dramatically. Seems like you're sweet and innocent while attending elementary school. When you take the step up to intermediate school, you meet kids from other areas and really start learning about things like swearing, theft, smoking, drinking, sex and attitude.

From time to time we used our secret path, riding skateboards and going under the compound by crossing through a maze of storm drains. We had a skateboard brigade that maneuvered through dark paths of underground storm drainpipes which always led us into and out of any area on the army base. It wasn't too long before we found an arsenal of weapons, including a real flame-thrower, hand grenades and other expensive toys like guns, ammunition and rockets. We had our own version of Special Forces back then. The thought never occurred to us that a flash flood could fill up these drainpipes. When you're young and dumb, things like that don't enter your mind.

One big risk we took was to cross into another section of drainpipes that traveled under the Diamond Head graveyard located next to our school and across from the Army base. We would be underground with our skateboards and one flashlight in a storm drain 300 yards long in the darkest, spookiest deadliest place surrounded by big rats, dead rats and spider webs. Buried above us were thousands of bodies. Maybe unknowingly, this was a test to see how mentally strong we were when put in this dark and confining situation. Would we panic and freeze halfway through this maze? Would our minds play tricks on us and suddenly see coffins and headless bodies in this dark tunnel? We did this a couple of times until the fun and challenge of it wore off. Little did I know that this test of my mental courage would confront me many times later in life under very serious circumstances.

Back in school things got interesting and my artistic talents expanded to architectural and mechanical drawings. Sometime around the eighth grade I showed an interest in signs and the art of letter styles. My bedroom was full of signs with nifty designs. The art of letter styles intrigued me so much I wanted to learn everything I could about painting signs with a brush and learning the art of freehand lettering.

For extra cash in school, I was the guy you came to if you needed to have a phony ID made to buy beer. If the big number on the safety check of your car bumper expired, I was the one who could change it. This worked out to be a great way to make extra lunch money.

One day we were on the slopes of Diamond Head Crater hanging out at one of our many secret camps, a bunker called Battery Harlow. The military police were always after us for trespassing but we were never caught except today, they had us trapped. We managed to elude them by running over the rim of the crater and into the shooting range hiding behind the targets during "live firing" exercises at the army base. Bullets were raining on us as we hid under the targets.

We were pinned down for hours until we could finally sneak out through a storm drain and go home. We were more afraid of being caught by the military police than of getting hit by all that gunfire.

As we grew older our toys were a lot more dangerous. Our neighborhood included Leahi Hospital next to the Army base. Between these two places we had access to chemicals and whatever we wanted. We were very crafty in building our own weapons, including bombs and other things that went BOOM! Our explosives were only meant to be competitive with the rival gang down the street. We would see whose bombs were the loudest, which had the strongest concussion and could make the deepest hole in the ground. We made high tech bow and arrows loaded with ammonia and sulfuric acid capsules. We used these when hunting wild boars and pigs. It was dangerous, because if we missed blasting the boar in the face, we got gored. This was living on the edge.

Our bomb making projects got more intricate and expanded to wild creations that we read about in a Popular Mechanics magazine. We built a catapult that could hurl a lighted, thousand pack roll of firecrackers over a hundred yards into the back yard of our competition down the street. Well, to retaliate, they countered back with a gatlin gun from plans they found in another magazine. They slaughtered us in a hail of pellets and BB's. There were times when our little bomb inventions blew up unexpectedly. One guy suffered serious burns. Other injuries were minor as someone slightly damaged an eyeball or an eardrum. A miracle at the right time was always there to save our young lives. Our parents never found out about our deadly games and that was a good thing.

During our young teenage years our transportation was the bus, our skateboards, bicycles or walking, so we didn't venture off more than five miles from our surroundings

Eventually, some of the older kids in our group were able to get their driver's license so this meant we could travel farther away from home and expand our horizons, like having a car and a few girls to join in the fun. I got my first job and bought my first car when I was 15, but my parents never found out about the cars I accumulated until I was 17, and by then they had no choice but to sign for my drivers license.

Maybe it's a good thing we turned our attention towards cars and girls because it took us away from the military base and Diamond Head and some of the dangerous things we got into. Of all the risky, dumb things we did as youngsters, this next incident had a hold on us long enough to scare us really good. Talk about a close call with death, this next story was almost our final. Do not try this at home because it would be a horrible way to die.

CHAPTER 4

DEATH TRAP
DIAMOND HEAD CRATER

I grew up just outside of Waikiki on the top of Monsarrat Avenue. This road borders the slopes of Diamond Head on the town side. At the top of this street you'll find the old Fort Ruger Theater, Leahi Hospital, a neighborhood store called Ruger Market and the Fort Ruger Army National Guard Base. If you were to follow this road around the crater the street name changes to Diamond Head Road and leads you to a breath taking view of the ocean and the beaches below. Real estate in this area includes the very high end, areas of Black Point and Kahala. Numerous high-ranking citizens of our fair state live here in this mega-bucks community that includes the very private ocean front estate called Cromwells.

Also known as Shangri-La, this is the lavish estate of Doris Duke a mega- billionaire who spent many years living in Hawaii. She and her first husband, James Cromwell, began construction on the estate in 1935 that included a private pier next to her ocean front property known simply as "Cromwell's." Back in the day, Doris Duke enjoyed sailing canoes and was often seen sailing out of Cromwell's, heading around Diamond Head and into Waikiki Beach a short distance away. Today it's still a favorite swimming, fishing and surfing spot for local youngsters and surfers.

Our gang had a secret hideout in an underwater cave, a lava tube next to the local swimming area where Cromwell's is located. The only way into this cave was at low tide when the ocean is very calm. We entered by swimming a short distance under a ledge, into the lava tube and then ended up in a giant cavern that led deep inside the sea cliffs. It was always pitch black and flashlights or candles were always necessary. One day this hideout turned into a death trap for my two friends and I because we nearly drowned.

While hanging out in this dungeon one day, we had no idea the weather outside went from good to really bad. Without warning, a huge wave plowed into the small opening filling up the entrance to our cavern. Another wave followed and it was bigger than the first. We were trapped as the seawater filled the cave.

Our panic cries and desperate yelling went unheeded. We thought we were all going to die in this underwater tomb and our bodies would never be found. Within a minute the water level receded a little and we were able to take a breath. Panic set in again as the water level began to rise cutting off our air supply. It was pitch black and all you could hear were our cries of desperation and then silence as the ocean water kept rising. There was a split second to say a prayer when calmness came over me. I prayed God was watching over us, and my belief became strong that we would be able to survive this ordeal. Without fail, something told me, "Stay calm. Don't be afraid."

It was impossible to stay calm, yet the message came to me again and again. We were in a desperate situation. We were going to drown. We tried to swim towards the entrance of the dark cave but the rushing water kept us from moving forward. We were trapped. The sharp edges of the lava walls cut up my arms and legs as the swirling waters pushed us around like we were in a mad washing machine. All of a sudden the water started going out really fast like someone next thing I knew, I was tossed out into a growling ocean.

I was struggling to breathe and to make it to the rocky cliffs when I noticed something was wrong. I was alone. My friends were nowhere to be seen. Panic came over me as I searched the ocean and called their names. My biggest fears started to mount when they couldn't be found. My only thought was they were still trapped in the cave. Without hesitating, I dove under the ledge and went back in. The next big wave caught me and I was swept into this underwater death hole. Instantly I was tossed around like a rag doll in a washer. Swimming to the top of the cave was the only thing to do. I needed to breathe and luckily there was a small pocket, just enough for me to get a quick breath of air. If it weren't for that, I would have drowned right there.

During all this I was able to make a pass around the inside of the cave and I didn't feel any bodies or hear any yelling. Not wanting to spend another second in there, I made it to the entrance where I could feel the water starting to empty out. Again I was scraped against the sides of the cave entrance and tossed out into the angry ocean. When I surfaced, I was alone. My friends were gone. I made it to the side of the cliff, caught my breath and started crying. Climbing up the rocks was really hard because I was pretty badly beaten up. As I lay on the top of the ridge, sounds of talking and crying were coming from a distance. It was my two friends crying because they thought I had drowned. When we saw each other we hugged and cried together. Turns out, when we were swept out of the cave the first time, they were carried further out to sea and finally made it to shore about two hundred yards down the beach.

They couldn't believe it when I told them I went back into that death trap to look for them. I asked, "Why not? Wouldn't you do the same thing for me?" They both

Doris Dukes estate, Shangri-La and Crownwells a popular local beach.

'X' marks the underground lava tube, that we permanently closed.

laughed and said, "What? No way!" With that we walked away arm in arm. A few days later we went back to the cave with one thing in mind. We took our homemade explosives and blew up the entrance to shut the cave permanently so other kids would never find this place.

This experience was a turning point for me. The Voice that was always there in times of danger enabled me to survive. I never told anyone about this gift for fear that it might disappear forever. At the same time it was evident that God had his Angels working overtime to watch me. He never gave up because He had a plan for me, I still had to figure out how to work it into my life.

When I was sixteen it was time for me to take it to another level and answer the call. This would be my first big test and it would be a very risky rescue. The conditions were not in my favor and the person in trouble is someone I don't know. I'm not a lifeguard and definitely not trained to do this kind of rescue. Are you ready to jump into this next situation with me? Grab your fins and follow me, if you dare to.

CHAPTER 5

Waikiki Surf Club's koa canoe Malia, the mother of all canoes.

ONE GUTSY MOVE

HAWAII'S TEAM SPORT - OUTRIGGER CANOE RACING

Outrigger canoe racing, the official "team sport" of Hawaii has grown immensely since its beginnings in the early nineteen hundreds. Back then only a handful of canoe teams would gather for informal races. Twenty to thirty-five foot canoes were dug out of logs from Koa trees and carried as few as two paddlers to as many as six.

Today canoe racing has grown to attract teams from around the world. In Hawaii alone, there are at least sixty-five canoe clubs participating in races throughout the state between the March and September canoe season. High schools have picked up canoe racing as a team sport and since 1994 at least twenty-five schools with over 1000 paddlers participate during their January to March racing season. While koa canoes are still being raced, fiberglass canoes have become plentiful in Hawaii and elsewhere. The length of a racing canoe is now up to 45 feet.

The canoe-racing season is brought to a close by the *"Big Race"*, the annual Molokai to Oahu channel crossing. This race is considered the *"Super Bowl"* of canoe races. Held every year since 1952, the event attracts worldwide participants. In the first year, the winning time for this thirty-eight mile open ocean crossing of the Molokai Channel was just under nine hours. Now winning teams complete this same race in less than five hours. Only three teams entered the race in 1952, but today the popularity and prestige of the event has grown to attract as many as one hundred teams.

A DREAM COME TRUE

In 1966, I paddled for Waikiki Surf Club and was the captain of our "16 and under" crew when I was invited to ride on the escort boat as a helper in the Molokai race. I danced with excitement because this would be my very first trip across the Molokai Channel, one of the roughest channels in the world. This chance for a kid like me to hang with the big boys of Waikiki Surf Club was a dream come true. Being introduced to the race was a highlight of my young paddling career and needless to say, I jumped at the opportunity to see what paddling the Molokai Channel was like. In a few years time my turn would come to be a paddler in this big event.Waikiki Surf Club was definitely the team to beat, as it had won the race many times. They entered two teams for this race, one crew would be paddling in a fiberglass canoe and their top crew would be using their classic koa racing canoe, the "Malia". Each team consisted of nine paddlers. Six would be in the canoe at one time with three relief paddlers resting on the escort boat.

I started paddling with the club when I was in the seventh grade. Our coaches at the time were Dutchy Kino, Nappy Napoleon and Big Blue Makua. They looked me over the very first day I turned out for practice. I was a skinny, lanky twelve-year old who ended up being chosen to be the steersman and captain for our "12 and under" crew.

Waikiki Surf Club's old style, long and hard stroke.

Talk about pressure and stress, I had to learn fast because these coaches saw something in me. These guys were the best canoe paddlers and steersmen to learn from. They taught me well and it paid off in the years to come. The difference between winning and losing almost always comes down to the abilities of the steersman of your crew. Over the next thirty-seven years, canoe racing became an integral part of my life as I embraced opportunities to become a steersman, waterman and canoe builder.

PREPARING FOR THE RACE OF 1966

To get to Molokai, we rode on a big fifty-foot craft that became the escort boat for the race back. Back in this time there were only big escort boats. We didn't have the leisure of smaller boats like the Whalers or Radon's and Glass Pros. On any given day, the Molokai Channel can be as smooth as glass with no wind and no clouds, and at other times it can be bumpy, choppy and downright rough and nasty. We left Oahu Friday morning and headed into an already nasty ocean. The channel was roaring and the forecast said it would get worse.

Seasickness engulfed me for the first and last time in my life. I was sick for most of the ten hours that it took to get to Molokai. Being the only kid on board, I was subject to the friendly teasing of the older crewmen, all seasoned fishermen. During the entire trip, they showed no mercy poking fun at me. We finally arrived at Hale O Lono, a tiny harbor sandpit on the west-end of Molokai. This little hole in the wall comes to life each year for the big Molokai to Oahu canoe race.

Our first evening meal was fish that had been caught on the way to Molokai. With my stomach being virtually empty, I felt as though I could eat anything and everything. Fortunately, my bout with the ocean had come to an end. I was able to get a good night's sleep and woke the next day feeling just fine. While some of our crew dove for lobster, the rest of us began the task of rigging the canoes and preparing for Sunday's race.

To keep the ocean from pouring into the canoe, a canvas spray cover is fitted over the top of the canoe. The outriggers are lashed to the canoe with cords measuring about one hundred feet in length. This is a very crucial part of the rigging process. If not done correctly, the performance of the canoe will be tipsy at best and will contribute to a long and frustrating day at sea. Proper rigging enables the crew to concentrate on paddling and to not be concerned about the possibility of the canoe flipping over. I was very fortunate to be part of this important preparation process. The techniques developed by each club are precious and well guarded by club members. Back in those days, there could be a certain amount of tampering by adding or removing weights from the canoe. The official weight requirement for each canoe is four hundred pounds. By Saturday night our crew was ready for the race. We were anxious for the upcoming dual against

Racing canoe with a canvas spray cover.

man and nature.

Following dinner of lobster and fish caught by our fishing crews, some of us wandered over to check out the festivities and mingle with the locals. The people of Molokai swarm to this evening event that is part of the annual Aloha Week Festival. Everyone participates in the festivities with music, hula, and food for all. It's a great party and an excellent prelude to the main event. Finally, we all fell asleep next to our canoes, with the stars in the deep dark sky keeping watch over all.

In the early years of this race, canoe clubs slept by their canoes on the beach the night before the big race.

THE DAY OF THE RACE

Sunday morning came much too soon. We gathered our teams together for a final look at the race plan. I nearly choked with excitement as I stood there listening to coach Nappy Napoleon say these words to all of us, "Today the channel is smoking and everybody is going to have to be on top of their game. The escort boat and crew will have their work cut out for them. Today the name of the game is survival. Be safe. Keep mistakes to a minimum, and bring the canoes and yourselves home safely. If all goes as planned, we could win again. Good luck and do your best!"

A prayer was said for all participants of the twelve teams. Then each club had its own private gathering to be one with God and to ask for blessings of strength, wisdom and safe passage. Our two crews made their way to the starting line, outside Hale O Lono Harbor. The winds at the start of the race were clocked at eighteen knots and expected to increase as we got further into the channel.

Waikiki Surf Club's Senior Mens Team was the one to beat this year. They had won this race many times, not only because they blended well as a crew but also because they possessed the "mother" of all canoes, the *"Malia."* She was the most beautiful and fastest koa canoe of the time. Our second crew, also excellent paddlers and watermen, would be using a brand new fiberglass canoe. What a grand slam it would be if both crews would finish first in their respective divisions!

The team from Kailua Hawaiian Civic Canoe Club, with their beautiful koa canoe, sat next to us. The men of the Outrigger Canoe Club were ready with their koa canoe, hoping to defend their title as winners of last year's channel crossing. It was very clear that these champions were out to make it a "back to back" win. Other teams entered included the Maile Sons from Leeward Oahu, and Molokai's team the Hawaiian Athletic Canoe Club, and the Order of Kamehameha all had their crews ready to do battle with the raging ocean that lay ahead.

Lanikai Canoe Club from windward Oahu, the team that took first place in the fiberglass division the year before, had both Koa and fiberglass canoes entered. Hui Nalu Canoe Club of Oahu was another club entering canoes in both divisions. Healani Canoe Club of Oahu had a single entry in the fiberglass division.

The stage was set for the most brutal, physically demanding, exhausting water sport ever to take place. No one knew what waited out in that angry sea, especially me, a young teenager along for the experience of his first open ocean channel crossing. Little did I know my physical and mental abilities would be put to a test. Today it would be life or death for me, a time to stay calm and survive, or to die in a rage of panic.

"Boom." The resounding blast of dynamite signaled the start of the race, and at last the competition was on. Almost immediately, Waikiki Surf Club's first crew went ahead of the pack and settled down for what would be a long day. The adrenaline was pumping in me with every stroke of their paddles. Excitement overwhelmed me, because I was there at the big dance with the ocean.

A sprint to the Laau Point would bring us into the channel. The game plan was to increase the distance from the other canoes and to take advantage of the smoother waters

Waikiki Surf Club mid-channel between Molokai and Oahu

by staying close to the shoreline of Molokai. Soon we would be passing Laau Point, rushing into one of the most feared channels in the world. It was living up to its angry status and we looked forward to some big time rock n' roll.

As expected, the channel was roaring. Fifteen to twenty-foot swells were all you could see. White caps caused by ocean spray blowing in horizontal sheets and steep troughs between swells, created misery for all in only the first couple of hours. Visibility being limited, it was difficult to tell where our first crew was located. We had radio contact with them making it easier to stay on the same course.

Seasickness almost revisited me once again while riding an ocean that wasn't all that calm, but I prayed for relief and focused on my role. My job was to help the paddlers climb aboard the escort boat, and to provide them with oranges and water or juice. The paddlers were exhausted, the condition of the ocean being a great contributor to their weariness.

Back in the day, the classic race was the "Leilani", Outrigger Canoe Club's koa canoe against the "Malia", Waikiki Surf Club's koa canoe.

Six paddlers are in the canoe at any given time. The relief paddlers jump from the escort boat to take their places. This is called *"making a change"*. Three men jump into the water and try to stay in line with the canoe that is heading straight for them. Seats or positions to be relieved have already been pre-determined. As the canoe reaches a certain point close to the men in the water, three paddlers from the canoe jump out on the right side of the canoe. At the same time the relief guys jump into the canoe from the left side. There should be no stopping or stalling if this maneuver is done correctly. The paddlers who are not being relieved do not miss a stroke and the relief paddlers pick up the pace with no interruption. This is a slick maneuver when done right.

Making changes in treacherous conditions demands tremendous physical stamina. Changes are made fifteen or twenty times during the thirty-eight mile race. Following the changes, the escort boat circles back to retrieve the paddlers who have been waiting to be picked up. Completing the drop off and retreating to pick up the other paddlers takes a while.

In the meantime our canoe continues on its way and vanishes from sight because of the big ocean swells caused by this nasty storm. During the race, the fight for survival in ocean conditions seemed to grow from bad to worse with every passing moment. Stamina and strength dwindled quickly.

About three and a half hours into the race we made another routine approach to pick up our three guys in the water. A huge swell pushed the escort boat directly over them. I feared the props had eaten them up as we passed over. Immediately the captain slammed the transmission into neutral. That pause separated us from the paddlers, and separated them from one another. We had to circle again.

In a few moments we saw two paddlers trying to swim to our boat just when another monstrous swell separated us from the paddlers. They disappeared. The third fellow was missing. Confusion set in. Voices were calling for help in different directions. Was it one person or three calling for help? For a fast second we found the lone paddler just before a giant ocean swell crashed down on him. Our captain tried placing the boat as close as possible to the paddler, but the high seas pulled us further away. As we drifted away he grew weaker, seemingly able to only tread water and rapidly losing the strength to swim. It was a serious situation.

I was on the back transom trying to reach out for the paddler and watched helplessly as we were pulled apart once again by the swells. I yelled to our captain, "He's not going to make it. Somebody has to jump in and get him." Something had to be done or he would lose his life. In another second a bigger set of waves drilled this already battered man. Softly I heard a voice saying, *"You can do it, go save him."*

Our crew consisted of mostly older seasoned fishermen who were not physically in shape to attempt a rescue. I found them all staring at me. One of them said, *"Boy you gotta go get him or else he no going make it."* Being the youngest on board and in fairly good shape for a sixteen-year old I knew there was no other choice. I grabbed the life ring and my fins and headed for the back of the boat when the captain called out that he was going to find the other two paddlers. This meant I would have to find the lone paddler and remain in the water until he could come back for us. This would turn out to be a big mistake. Again I was reassured by that silent voice, "You can do it, go get him."

Growing up in Hawaii, I was used to moderate surf and knew how to handle myself against the powers of the sea. This would be my first time in the middle of the Molokai Channel and conditions were not in my favor. Twenty-foot seas, thirty-five knot winds, a storm tossed ocean, a complete white out. Was I ready for this, my first open ocean rescue? My fears whipped before me like the raging wind because I might never see this escort boat again. I'm a risk taker, but doing this was beyond my limits.

Screams from the paddler brought me back to reality. He needed help and he needed it now. His screams were silenced as another gigantic wave crashed upon him. With my fins on and the life ring trailing behind me, I dove over the side of the boat. God help us. My hope was that he would still be treading water even though I knew his limits had been reached.

As I swam ahead, the escort boat vanished behind another swell. I was alone. The sea was pounding me with tremendous force. Waves broke from all directions. Each time I dove under a wave, the life ring would yank me back up again. Gusts of wind produced white caps that surrounded me with a wall of fear. Getting slammed by the elements wasn't fun. I would be lost at sea if things didn't get better. I was being slammed by the large ocean swells. The current was kicking in and pulling me away fast. There were no sounds of life around me. Trying to survive while looking for him was tough. I had to keep pushing on and started to wonder:

Was this a mistake to try and save this person without the aid of the escort boat?
Would it be worse if we made the other guys wait until we found this one fellow?
What would you have done? What if it was you in the water needing help?
So many questions, and no time to think.

Looking up, the dark overcast clouds showed signs of distress. Will I be lost at sea all because I made the choice to help someone in serious trouble? By all accounts I should have panicked and cried for help too. The most important thing to do was to stay calm and not choke on the salt water.

Yeah, right! Try doing that while Mother Nature constantly pounds you with fifteen to twenty foot seas. I was counting the intervals between each wave. Twelve seconds before I had to dive under each wave. Eventually doing this gets you weak. I knew I had to use my energy wisely. The wind speed intensified and the sounds of a full-blown storm at sea were enough for me to give in and die. Reality set in. I was lost at sea and chances of survival were remote. At least I had my fins and the life ring. If anything I could swim to Hawaii Kai, which was only fifteen miles away. Yeah right!

Then right on cue that voice came to me in a soft distinct tone. "Relax and don't be afraid, you can do this, stay calm." Over and over I heard the message. Finally an overwhelming feeling of calmness surrounded me. My panic and feelings of distress subsided. I listened intently to the Voice. Someone was watching over me. Everything would be okay.

With a sudden surge of energy I was able to concentrate and focus on finding the paddler. The seas were growling at me and grinding up my strength. Still I swam on ducking under every wave that pounded me with no mercy. But no luck, the paddler was gone. Not a sound could be heard from him.

Then, just as I was about to change directions and look in another area, I spotted my target. He was still afloat, but weakening rapidly and he was down to doing the final "death dance" which is brought on by shear panic. He never saw me coming as I sneaked up from his blind side. I was able to get the life ring around him, although he made every attempt to pull both of us under time and time again.

Instantly, a giant ocean swell pounded us and we were separated. Eventually I found him again. His panic had subsided. He was doing okay. Assuring him that we would be saved, I encouraged him to not fight my efforts. I wanted him to salvage what little strength he had left. I hoped I could do as much for myself. He asked about the escort boat. I told him the captain had to pick up the other two paddlers. I sensed him beginning to panic so I didn't tell him how long I had been stranded before I found him.

Twenty minutes passed and still no sign of the escort boat. It would be hard for the boat to spot us since we were only two heads bobbing in the storm tossed seas. I wish I had thought to bring flares. We were getting a pretty good lashing by the ocean. Luckily I had the fins to make it easier to dive under the waves. My focus was to keep him in the life ring, and to not risk another separation from each other.

Waikiki Surf Club's "Malia", seconds after this photo was shot, a 20 foot wave came up on their right side, flipping the canoe to the left, over the outriggers.

*Winners of 1966 Molokai Canoe Race, Waikiki Surf Club.
Nappy Napoleon, Randy Chun, Micheal Tongg, Richard Henning,*

This was the worst and biggest channel crossing ever in history.
Jeff Young, Val Ching, Blue Makua Jr., Nick Beck and Rabbit Kekai.

Did I do the right thing or will we be lost at sea after all?

Out of nowhere the escort boat came into view. I swam with the exhausted paddler clinging to the life ring. The pick up would be difficult in the storm-ravaged seas. To maneuver the boat close enough to us was going to be tricky. My prayers were with the captain. I had to trust him to do the right thing at the right time.

All at once a strange calm came over the water, a mysterious settling of the elements, just long enough for the captain and crew to haul us out of the ocean. When we were safely on board, Mother Nature resumed her overture.

What force had caused these drastic changes so quickly and so fleetingly? The thought passed through my mind and exited into the unknown. As unbelievable as it seemed, I knew something powerful had just taken place right before my eyes. Someone calmed the ocean down to enable us to get back on the escort boat safely.

After we got on the boat, I was exhausted and needed to sit for a while. My life ring passenger said nothing to me. But he repeatedly thanked the captain and crew for finding him. This was a slap in the face experience that I will never forget. This fellow acted as if he were embarrassed because a young teenage kid had come to his aid. The remaining time spent on the escort boat with him was weird. He ignored me and never expressed his thanks when the race was over. Something was wrong with this picture.

The captain turned to me and said, "That was one gutsy move for a kid to make, that paddler surely would have drowned had it not been for you." I asked the captain what took so long. He responded by saying, "We lost you guys. It wasn't until something told me to head in a certain direction that we found you."

Our canoe team was long gone and needed to be found quickly. Reports from the first crew told us they were having problems too. The mighty ocean had already capsized their canoe three times. Trying to right the canoe took about fifteen minutes every time they went over. In paddling terms this is called a swamping or a flip. It is possible to get your canoe right back up again providing your water tight canvas cover hasn't broken. We still had over an hour to go before we would reach the finish line at Waikiki and the time went by fast without any glitches, but survival was still the key word.

By the time the race was coming to an end the picture was easier to see. The final mile was in the calm waters off Diamond Head. Out of the twelve crews that entered the race, only six canoes finished the treacherous course. The six remaining canoes that did not cross the finish line had their problems. Two koa canoes were split apart, destroyed and lost in the mighty ocean. Two other canoes had to be towed back to Molokai after they got in trouble early in the race. The last two canoes were towed into Hawaii Kai on Oahu. Several escort boats got in trouble along the way and many paddlers

Glassy conditions prevailed in this 1989 channel crossing with Imua Canoe club from Newport Beach, California, using the canoe "Eddie Aikau."

and helpers suffered from seasickness, exhaustion or were lost at sea for a long time before being found. This 1966 race was the worst of the worst ever to be recorded for a channel race.

Outrigger Canoe Club's Senior Masters at the finish line, Molokai race.

Waikiki Surf Club's first crew won the race in their koa canoe. Their time was a long and hard six hours thirty-seven minutes. Their canoe, the *Malia*, had survived three swampings during the thirty-eight mile race. Second place went to the fiberglass crew of the Healani Canoe Club. These guys flipped over three times and managed to finish in fine standings. Third place was the team from Molokai followed by Lanikai's fiberglass entry and close behind was our crew from the Waikiki Surf Club. Finishing sixth place was the Hui Nalu team in their Koa canoe.

Days later I sat on the wall at the Diamond Head Lookout watching the ocean, and looking at Molokai on the horizon almost forty miles away. I was mad at myself for doing such a dangerous rescue. I could have drowned. I was unhappy with the outcome because the fellow I saved did not talk to me, shake my hand, give thanks or acknowledge his close call with death. *"I'll never do something like that again, risk my life for someone I don't know."* This was my only thought as I stared at the foaming windswept sea rolling past the lookout.

Moments later a tour bus opened its doors and visitors were walking all around the lookout. An older man in a casual off-white outfit stood close to me and fumbled with his camera trying to take some pictures. I could tell he was fascinated by what he saw. He watched the surfers dancing on the silvery waves below and focused on the distant horizon. Without looking at me, he began to speak in a soft tone.

"You were watched over and kept safe, you answered the call and did well. As your life goes on, you will be a giving person, ready to help anyone. Don't expect anything in return and if things don't work out, don't hold it against anyone. You are blessed with many gifts, use them. Your Father has plans for you."

After that, he turned and walked away. I was shocked from this surprise. My reaction was negative but I kept it to myself. *"Who the heck is this clown? He comes out of nowhere. He knew exactly what was bugging me and told me my Father has plans for me. What does my Dad have to do with this?"*

He was gone as mysteriously as he appeared. I looked around and he had vanished, maybe with that tour bus that was pulling away. Being a young teenager, and not knowing about Angels, I shook off the incident and walked away. Someone should have given me a slap upside the head. It would be years later before I realized who that messenger was.

The next two years my goal was to survive high school and graduate. My artistic talent could go in any direction, but I wanted to learn how to apply gold leaf and paint signs on race cars with a brush and I wanted to design and fabricate signs. I already had the hotrods, motorcycles and girls. I wasn't aware of what my calling would be in life and more and more incidents like this last one started to happen on a regular basis. At eighteen, my life went in a different direction and this gift would follow me wherever I went. So pack your bags because we're moving to Southern California.

CHAPTER 6

SELECTIVE HEARING

1968 was a dark year in American history. Dr. Martin Luther King Jr. and Robert Kennedy were shot down and cities across America were on fire because of Civil Rights riots. The Viet Nam War took a major turn with the Tet Offensive as the North Vietnamese Army pulled off an all-out assault on every South Vietnamese city and all American bases, all at the same time. Our military won the battle but America's popularity with the war dropped rapidly especially following the Mi Lai Massacre.

Anti-war riots were everywhere. Resistance, protest, and revolutions were going on from coast to coast. President Johnson saw no way out of the war and decided not to run for another term in office. The top brass in Washington wanted a major call up of men for the military. They were asking for two hundred thousand more men. President Johnson activated the National Guard into the war but still they needed more men.

By June of 1968 I was 18 and would be graduating from high school and most likely get drafted by the Selective Service into the Army if I didn't join up with another military branch. By then our class song was:

"And it's 1,2,3, what are we fighting for?
Don't ask me, I don't give a damn.
Our next stop is Viet Nam."

Most of my classmates and friends had already joined the military and after graduation everybody would be off to boot camp and eventually end up in Nam. Two weeks after graduation from high school in 1968, I split to Southern California. Back then a one-way ticket to Los Angeles on Pan American was only $88. I sold my hot rod cars, collected money from uncles, aunties and other family members and left Hawaii.

I had two choices. My first option was to take advantage of an art scholarship at a small college in Southern California. If I went to college I could sidestep the draft and the war in Viet Nam. The second choice was to join the Navy, see the world and probably the war. Eventually my plans got put aside during this young time in my life because of my *"new found lifestyle in California."* My thoughts on the war were simple. If the Selective Service found me, I would go willingly but I forgot to notify them of my new address in California. I wasn't protesting the war, nor was I running from it. I was just sidestepping the draft until they caught up with me.

My new lifestyle in Southern California was a constant party. This was the War Bashing, flower power era with hippies, hash pipes, black lights, young aggressive women, old whiskey, Spanada wine and fast Harleys. It was the days of rock and roll with Creedence, the Jefferson Airplane, Steppenwolfe, Canned Heat, Three Dog Night and the Stones. Merl Haggard and Johnny Cash kicked up the country stuff while Hendrix, Janice, Dylan, and the Greatful Dead caused us to have some hazy memories. Then the climax was the long seventeen-minute version of In-a-Gadda-da-Vida. You should have been there. I did some time in the middle of San Francisco's Haight-Ashbury district and back in Los Angeles I took a job on Sunset Boulevard working at Hollywood's top strip club called the Pink Pussy Cat. On the other side of the world a war was going on and it would only be time before the government would find me.

In the summer of 1969 I got that "knock on the door." It was two FBI agents looking for me. In one hand they had a letter, a draft notice to report for a physical in Los Angeles. In the other hand was a set of handcuffs. *"Son, it's your choice, take this letter and show up on this date or put on these cuffs and come with us."* For me the party was over. I would be heading to the U.S. Army and by now I was ready to go to war. On my appointed day I cut my hair, shaved the beard and side burns and showed up at some building in L.A. to stand in line with all kinds of characters. There were a lot of long-haired freaky types, Honkies and Red Necks, Mexicans and Blacks, Criminals and Atheists, Geeks and Nerds, Fags and Transvestites. I was the only one from Hawaii so this was quite a culture shock for me.

During the physical they seemed to have concentrated on my hearing a lot more than for the other guys. *They kept saying, "What's wrong with your hearing?"* I'd say, "WHAT?" Again they would ask me and I'd respond, "WHAT?" *"Go follow the yellow line down to the end of the hall, we need to test your ears."* So I followed the line to a sound proof booth and did more testing. Seriously they asked me if I had any problems hearing and I said my hearing was fine, but when I was a young kid my mom used to ring my ears a lot and when I was in high school I was a drummer in a rock and roll band. That wasn't good enough for them and they sent me following another yellow line down the hall to do more tests again.

When they were done making me follow yellow lines they sat me down in an office and said they were sorry but I wasn't going to pass the draft physical because I didn't pass the hearing test. I was shocked. One young Army medic pulled me aside and said I had something called *Selective Hearing*. "I have what?" Here I was in perfect health, 6' tall, 185 pounds, zero percent body fat and they cut me. I was pissed.

I had to sign a bunch of papers, initial here and there, and in the end, I was classified 1-Y, "Only to be drafted in case of a national call up." When I left the building I was stunned at being turned down from this physical and yet I knew there were other young guys in that building who would kill to be in my position.

On this day, thousands across our nation were protesting the war in Viet Nam, while our young men were dying in that far off land for whatever reasons no one could understand. I felt let down because I was turned away knowing that I could have made a difference with my selective hearing gift, if I was drafted and sent to Nam. I thought this gift that allowed me to hear a "pre-warning message of danger," was a great asset to have, but the military called my selective hearing a bad thing and turned me away. It took me a few days to get over this let down.

As the years went on I was able to learn to trust and respect this certain voice that always seemed to find me, no matter where I was. If I traveled to the Far East, South Pacific, or across the 48 states and Canada, it was always there to warn me of danger. It's omnipotent, strong and at the same time, silent but effective. It has calmed me in the moments prior to panic and death situations so I could survive. When called upon, I would react to it, even if it meant putting my life on the line to rescue some stranger. If the call said to jump into the fire, I did. If I was asked to jump into a storm tossed ocean to help a stranger, I did and the list goes on and on.

During my young life while growing up in Hawaii, I wasn't into religion. Going to church on Sundays was not my choice and Mom had to drag me to Sunday school at the

Mormon Church even though I had no interest in learning about religion. At an early age my parents taught me about respect for others, to be kind and understanding to all of my friends and people I met and they taught me about God and Jesus.

Things changed for me when I was around 22 years old in Southern California. Early one Sunday morning I was out roller skating in Costa Mesa where I was living and came up to the intersection of Sunflower and Fairview. There was a big strawberry field and an empty lot with a large brown Army tent. It was as big as a circus tent and my curiosity told me to find out what was going on under that canopy. At first I thought it was an auction. Then I noticed people dressed in suits and their Sunday best, so I skated up to this tent and a fellow at the door waved at me to come inside. I was hesitant because of how I was dressed, tank top, shorts, baseball cap and roller skates. He assured me that Jesus didn't care how I was dressed and led me inside to my seat. A fellow named Chuck Smith was speaking and this temporary tent was the new location for a church called Calvary Chapel, Costa Mesa. What that speaker said was meant for me to hear. It was Jesus knocking at the door to my heart and I was finally ready to let him in.

Within a year, I would be called on again to do a daring rescue. Would I be ready mentally and physically or would I hold back because I was afraid of dying? Again, I find myself in a deadly situation attempting to rescue someone I don't know. This rescue almost did me in but luckily someone was there to help us survive.

CHAPTER 7

RAPID REACTION
THE COLORADO RIVER IN ARIZONA

In the story, "One Gutsy Move," It was 1966 and I dove into a situation that probably could have cost me my life while attempting to save a stranger from drowning in rough seas. It was daring and stupid, but I did it, not knowing that I was purposely put into that situation to answer a call to save someone. Well, in 1973 I got that call again.

I was 23 when my two friends and I drove from Orange County, California to a campsite in Arizona where the Colorado River attracts thousands of college kids on vacation during long holiday weekends. The atmosphere at the river was a constant 24-hour party with fast boats, good whiskey and lots of young women. During the summertime, the temperature burns hot at 110 degrees so all the action is in the river. Ski boats, drag boats, floating beer bars, and people on rafts or inner tubes spread across the river, making this a very crowded and exciting place. At night, it cools off to 85 degrees and the usual activity is camping by the river's edge. There are barges on the river that turn into nightclubs making for a fun time dancing the night away. I made several trips to this area over the years and it was always the same scene, Party, Party, Party.

This particular trip turned out to be something different. We decided to set up camp at the edge of the river just downstream from a rough section of rapids. The river comes down from a dam about a mile away and makes a big sweeping turn, allowing the water to turn into a fast moving current at the edge of the shoreline. The rapids in this section were passable only by raft, kayak or inner tube. It was Sunday and we had been there for two days and it looked like we wouldn't head home until Tuesday. I was trying to catch up on some rest after the last two nights of partying, so I decided to hang around the campsite and watch all the action on the river. It was a wonder people didn't get hurt or killed on the river with all the ski boats towing water skiers, drag boats, cabin cruisers, and houseboats going in every direction. Adding to all of this were the people floating on rafts and inner tubes, or paddling along in kayaks and canoes. There probably was an accident every now and then, but I had never witnessed one on any of my trips.

It was about 2 p.m. humid, sticky and hot. Next to our campsite were highway patrol officers seemingly intent on harassing a large group of college kids. Upstream a lot of people were floating down the river on rafts and inner tubes with cases of beer tied to it. I noticed a girl on an inner tube coming downstream dangerously close to the rough rapids where the river makes its sweeping turn. She was having a good time cruising along with the current and not paying attention to the dangers ahead. Right about this same time a message was coming to me. It was that familiar Voice telling me, "Help this girl, she's heading for trouble, help her." Again this warning was repeated to me over and over. "Help her." I opted to watch because it looked like she would be okay.

The commotion next to me was getting louder and it grabbed my attention. The Highway patrol officers were aggressively asserting their authority. People were being arrested. Fights started and it looked as if an all out brawl was about to start. More police arrived on the scene and it was obvious the situation was getting serious.

All of a sudden, there were screams and yelling coming

from upriver. It looked like someone was in trouble, so I ran over to check it out. It was the girl on the inner tube. She had been sucked between two small islands where the powerful rapids picked up speed along the river's edge. Between the riverbank and one of the islands, a big rope was stretched across at water level and was tied to a tree on each side. This rope provided a way to cross over to the island.

    This big line was just below the surface and the girl couldn't see it. The rope *"clothes lined"* the girl by the neck and swept her off the inner tube. The situation was critical. People were diving into the river trying to help her, but were washed away by the force of the rapids. More people tried in vain to reach the girl by clinging to the rope, but they kept getting washed away. I could see that a rescue was possible but it would be very risky. Two highway patrol officers were standing right there but it didn't look like they were going to do anything. Even if they called the fire department for help, it would be too late. Something had to be done now. The only way to save her would have to be now and well planned. I've done some high-risk things from time to time, but this one looked deadly. I always calculate what the risk entails before I jump into any situation, but this circumstance was different and could be fatal for me.

    I rehearsed my idea while running way upstream and planned my maneuver as I dove into the river. After diving in, I bodysurfed the rapids straight for the girl. My plan was to get trapped with her. As I got closer, I wanted to aim for a spot where I might have my arms free so I could help her. It was a bold plan and I thought it was the only way to get to her. Then I realized this might not be a good idea. The force of the river was moving me at a very fast pace toward the rope. Out of nowhere, that familiar Voice was telling me, "Be calm, you can do it, be calm." I had thoughts about aborting the rescue attempt. I could easily go under the rope and pass right by this poor girl, but I wanted to take one good shot at right by this poor girl, but I wanted to take one good shot at helping her. I realized that the rope could cut my body in half. I was ready to chicken-out as I started to think, "This is a bad idea."

It was too late, the rapids swiftly pulled me to her and in a second I slammed into the rope right in the mid-section of my stomach. The force of slamming into the line was too much and it knocked the breath out of me. I almost blacked out. For a moment, I was curled over the rope with my head underwater and the full force of the river rushing over my body. I realized there might be two people dying here if I didn't take care of myself first. Slowly I regained control of the situation. Inch by inch, I positioned myself down into the water so that the rope was on my chest. I caught my breath and concentrated on helping the girl.

She had been underwater for a long time. I grabbed her head, pulled her up and saw that she wasn't breathing so I tilted her head back and I blew a mouthful of air into her. The rope had snagged tightly around her neck as I tried pulling her head above the water. Again, I blew a breath of air into her, hoping it was a breath of life. It felt like I was holding onto a dead girl. She was lifeless. The river didn't let up. The force was so strong. I didn't know how much longer I could take the pressure. The water was going over us so fast that it made matters worse. The situation got bad as I got weaker. I could see two highway patrol officers standing on the riverbank, not doing anything to help me. Other people were jumping in trying to help us, but got washed away downstream.

I continued giving her air and tried to free her from the rope. Water was filling my mouth and choking me. I couldn't hang on much longer. It was time for me to bail out. We were stuck. It seemed the river's power increased 10 times. I kept trying and trying, but the river was beating us. By now she was underwater again. The situation seemed fatal. I was growing weaker as I motioned to the people on the riverbank to get in the water downstream.

With my remaining strength, I said, *"Okay, you got me in this, now help us out."* A soft Voice instantly was assuring me, *"You will be okay, you can do it."*

I blew a big breath of air into her and at the same time, the whole scene seemed to move in slow motion. For a few seconds there was no pressure from the rapids as I pulled her head down with my left hand and pushed the rope away. With those precious seconds, we had the miracle I needed to get her loose. Now the river was at full force again. Her body was free from the rope and drifting down river, underwater.

All the people in the water were trying to find her and pull her in. I was trapped on the rope but it was no concern to me now. I waited to see if anyone would find her. The river's pressure was too overwhelming and I was exhausted. Emotionally I was drained, knowing I tried my best to save her life. I freed myself from the rope that had me trapped, floated downstream and made it to the riverbank, exhausted and trying to catch my breath.

Miracles happen when you least expect it. Miracles are the cause of a divine intervention by a supreme power when a human situation is in need. There was joyful yelling and cries of happiness coming from the riverbanks downstream. The girl was found and revived by CPR. I couldn't believe it as I walked down to her. I still couldn't believe it as I knelt down next to her. She was crying uncontrollably now, saying how she thought she was dead. I often wondered if this girl's life turned out okay for her. She definitely had an Angel with her that day. That was the last time I saw her.

CHAPTER 8

SURPRISE IN THE DARK
HONOLULU ZOO

It was January of 1983 and I had just returned to Hawaii from a bad winter driving my big rig across the nation's interstates. I was on vacation and planned to stay home, start up a small sign business and maybe go back to flying. One night I ran into an old friend, Herman, "Kimo," Kalahiki, a career fireman and driver trainer for Roberts Hawaii, the top tour bus company in the state. He made me an offer that was hard to refuse. "Hey come drive for Robert's, you get free dinners every night, drive air conditioned buses, wear a nice Aloha shirt, nice slacks and meet female tourists."

I was hesitant about driving a bus with passengers cause I never did something like that. Funny though, the last several months on the interstates, I was hauling Class A Explosives from Michigan to San Jose, California. That meant over the icy roads and up and down the Rocky Mountains through snow blizzards. I was right at home doing stuff like that, but drive a bus full of tourist people in Hawaii? I don't think so.

Well, the next day he set me up for a driving test on a tour bus. It was like driving a Volkswagon, compared to those big rigs I'm used to being in. I was hired that day. At the same time I started a small sign business and did the bus thing in the evenings.

The next story happened around 1985. I found myself

doing some things I usually don't do, and unknowingly several events were leading up to a surprise in the dark. I'm led to do things that I cannot explain, all starting with that same familiar voice talking to me. This story took place late one night at the Honolulu Zoo parking lot.

I was working evenings as a tour bus driver for Robert's Hawaii and it was about 9:30 p.m. I had just returned to Waikiki with a busload of tourists from one of the Hawaiian luaus held on the leeward coast of Oahu. After dropping off the tourists at their hotels I was cleared by the dispatcher to return to the base and call it a night. This was good, because there were a lot more dispatch orders for buses that night, mostly pick-ups and drop-offs at nightclubs and hotels around the Waikiki area.

There was one dispatch no driver wanted that particular night, an early morning departure from a Waikiki Hotel with drop off at the airport. The dispatcher was asking for a driver to take the 1:30 a.m. run. As I listened to the two-way radio, most of the drivers had an excuse for not taking the late trip to the airport. Usually new drivers got stuck with this type of late night run. I was already back at the base yard and the dispatcher was still on the radio looking for anyone to take the run. There was no way I would do it because I had a sign business that took up my daytime hours. No one wanted that 1:30 a.m. departure to the airport. Then softly, that familiar Voice was saying something to me, "Take that run. Take that run." I tried listening again for what I just heard, and the same thing was repeated, "Take that run. Do it now."

I was still in the bus when I picked up the microphone and told the dispatcher I would take the late dispatch. This was totally unusual for me to do because I was done for the night. After I put the microphone away, I said to myself,

"What the…? What did I do that for? Now what will I do for three hours?" Looking at my watch, it was almost 10:00 p.m. I figured I could drive back to Waikiki, and park somewhere. I couldn't believe what I had just done.

I continued turning the bus around to head back out again and kicking my self for volunteering to do this early morning job because it would be closer to 3 a.m. before I would get home and jump in bed. Just then I heard something faint. I heard a voice calling for help. My passenger bus was empty, but it sure sounded like it came from the back of the bus somewhere. I looked in my mirror to the back of the bus and it was empty so I headed back to Waikiki.

I had one good alternative. My lady friend lived in a condo unit just down the road from the hotel where my late night pick-up would be so I headed for her place right on the edge of Waikiki, directly across from the parking lot of the Honolulu Zoo. I knew I could drop in and visit any time I wanted to, and this would be a great way to spend the next three hours. Plus, there was a perfect spot to park the large tour bus right in front of her place. It was actually an illegal parking area, with a red curb. But hey, I had parked there many times before and never got a ticket. In order for me to get into this stall, I would have to turn into one entrance of the zoo parking lot, circle around, and come out the other exit, to be in a perfect position to fit into the illegal parking stall.

While cutting through the zoo parking lot, I heard that soft voice again. "Help me." It was faint but again it sounded like it was coming from the back of the bus. For some unknown reason, I pulled the bus over to the darkest corner of the parking area and stopped the bus there. I took a quick walk to the rear of the bus, searched every seat, and made my way back to the front. I shut down the engine and lights and locked the door, leaving the bus parked right next to the tall hedges that bordered the zoo. It was very dark in this area, with no lampposts around and I remember stepping off the bus thinking there might be a gorilla hiding in those bushes, ready to jump out and hold me hostage, as I drove him away so that he could escape. Highly unlikely, but a wild thought.

I walked away from the bus, crossed the street, and continued on to my friend's place. That voice I heard still did not alert me. The bus ended up one hundred yards away from the place where I usually park. I never gave it a second thought as to why I parked in that particular spot, except that I knew it would be better to park there. When I finally got upstairs, the first thing I did was call the dispatcher to let him know where I was and gave him the phone number just in case the job might be cancelled at the last minute. Checking on the bus, I looked out over the balcony to see the glittering chrome bumper and reflections from the windows, and it looked okay.

My friend asked, "Why is your bus so far away, and not downstairs where you usually park?" I told her I needed to park the bus for three hours and the zoo parking lot was a great place to put it, and I didn't know why I took this late night run. She was glad I showed up anyway, and the next three hours was spent watching the late news, Johnny Carson, and the David Letterman Show on television.

At about 12:45 a.m. I happened to look out over the balcony to check on the bus and noticed a car pulling away from the same dark area where the bus was parked. It was moving pretty fast, with no lights on, as it started to head up the street. Finally the headlights came on and the car disappeared in traffic. It was a large sedan, a late model silver Cadillac. Since the bus looked okay, I didn't give any more thought to the caddy.

Three hours went by fast and now it was almost 1:00 a.m. I decided to leave and take a walk back to the bus. After climbing into the bus I heard the same thing," Help me." Now I was alarmed. I put on the lights and walked to the back of the bus again looking for something, but no one was there. I decided to take care of my paperwork and fill out the dispatch sheet, instead of waiting until I got back to the bus yard. At the same time I kept thinking about that voice calling for help and I couldn't figure out what was going on. This reminded me of an old television show called, "One Step Beyond."

Completing most of the paperwork except for the bus inspection sheet, I stepped off the bus and took a quick walk around to make sure the tires were okay, and the lights were not burned out. The only light at the back of the bus was coming from the taillights giving off an eerie red glow that illuminated the bushes next to the bus.

Then something caught my attention. I got the chills and my arms were covered with goose bumps. Under the bushes next to the bus was a shimmering glow, a reflection from the red light shining as if it wanted to be seen. Looking closer I could make out an image of a gold bracelet. Then the red glow of light cast a shadow on a haunting sight. The bracelet was wrapped around someone's wrist. "YIPES!" I jumped back against the bus and let out a scream. I managed to calm down and stepped closer to the bushes pulling away some branches and there, stuffed under the hedges, was the body of a young blonde girl.

She was in her early twenties, fully clothed with her face badly beaten. I checked her pulse by the neck and it was faint. Her vital signs were gone, no signs of breathing, no chest movement and no sound. She had a few more minutes of life so I cleared her air passage, lifted her chin and checked for any sign of breathing. I wiped the area around her mouth and gave her a long and slow breath of air. I thought about running into the bus to radio the dispatcher for help, but our dispatch office closed at midnight. Time was important and she needed an ambulance.

Again, I gave her another breath of life and planned my next move. She needed help and I had to find it now. I ran about 50 yards to a busy street trying to find a police officer, but no luck. The zoo parking lot was generally a hangout for police at night, but none were around. A minute went by before I saw a police officer coming down the road driving one of those popsicle scooters. After waving him down, I told him about the girl and asked him to call for an ambulance. We rushed over to where the girl's body was and waited for the paramedics to arrive. The officer took down some information and I explained that I had to leave for an airport run by 1:30 a.m. I also mentioned the big silver caddy I had seen leaving the area. We examined the girl, and he recognized her as one of the hookers who worked the streets of Waikiki. He was surprised because he last saw her a few hours ago standing on a street corner. He figured that the big caddy belonged to either her pimp or maybe her last customer and they were able to stuff the body under the bushes that was hidden by my large bus. Within minutes the place was swarming with police and ambulance paramedics. According to them, this young girl was lucky to be found because she was close to dying.

With all the excitement going on I almost forgot to watch the time. Luckily the hotel was close by and within two minutes I was at the hotel. The tourists were ready to head out to the airport and their luggage had gone ahead on a baggage truck. That was good news for me because I didn't feel like swinging bags at all.

On my way to the airport I thought about all the

different circumstances that led to the girl's discovery. Was it all a bunch of coincidences? Maybe she had a parent or grandmother somewhere back in Idaho or Florida or wherever who had a bad feeling about this girl coming into some serious trouble. Maybe they started to pray for this girl's protection and I answered the prayers. Call it strange, weird, mystical or unexplainable, someone knew in advance about her upcoming misfortune and set me up to do a couple of things out of the ordinary so that this girl's life would not end under some bushes.

The next day a small article in the Police Beat section in the newspaper told of a young twenty-three year old female prostitute who was found in a Waikiki parking lot, badly beaten and unconscious. The news article said her condition had changed from serious to stable. I may have had a small part in this, but a power greater than us deserves the credit and praise. I never saw this girl again.

Are you ready for a trip? Well you'll need a passport because we're going to Hong Kong, China. The outcome of this next story left me baffled but alive. So grab your running shoes, try to keep up, but DON'T follow me.

CHAPTER 9

A NEAR FATAL MISTAKE

There were many times when a verbal warning came to me in the nick of time with a sense of urgency because either my life or someone else's would be in trouble if I didn't react quickly. Most of these quick warning and fast reaction stories were left out of this first volume because they were similar situations and each story involved vehicles either heading into a head on collision or being broadsided at high speed. One story involved another car dropping out of the sky and almost landing in the windshield of my car. It was an instant warning that made us move to the side and avoid certain death.

This next story has a little "addition" to the instant message that's directed at me. Besides the usual warning from that voice of authority, a little helping hand at the precise time saved my life. This story takes us to Hong Kong, China where I would be taking part in a dragon boat race. This would be the first time for the United States to send a team to China to participate in such an event.

Dragon Boats are canoes made out of teak and are very heavy. It takes twenty-four little Chinese crewmen to paddle a canoe that also carries a drummer and a steersman. This type of racing has been going on in Asia for 200 years and is as popular a sport in China, as our Super Bowl and World Series are to us in the States. Dragonheads are carved on the front of each thirty-foot canoe. Riding on the front of the Dragon Boat is a drummer with a large bass drum. His drum solo sets the pace for the paddlers in the canoe at 90 strokes a minute. That's a fast pace to keep up while paddling.

Back in 1979, the United States had the opportunity to participate for the first time in this traditional Chinese race, thanks to President Jimmy Carter who opened trade relations with China. A team of all-star canoe paddlers from Hawaii was formed to represent the United States in a Dragon Boat Race in Hong Kong. At our first meeting with the media, tourism officials and State department heads, the team of paddlers from Hawaii was introduced to represent our nation. Falling asleep from time to time, I woke up in the meeting to learn I was the captain for our Team USA.

The intention was to try out dragon boat racing and perhaps open doors for the rest of the world to participate in this type of race. At the same time we wanted to show the folks in China our Hawaiian hospitality and Aloha Spirit. Along with our All Star paddlers we brought dignitaries from Hawaii's travel industry and our local media to cover this event. Hawaiian Air provided airline passes for all and even added their own local musicians and hula dancers to entertain our new friends in Hong Kong. Our mission was successful and we were invited back the following year.

The average size for a small Chinese crewmember was 85 pounds and a little over four feet tall. Our crew of Hawaii paddlers averaged six feet tall and 185 pounds per person so we couldn't load the dragon boat with a full crew of 24 plus the drummer and the steersman. We were only able to seat fourteen paddlers before the canoe was in danger of sinking. On our first practice attempt in the Dragon Boat, a wake from a passing tugboat washed across our low decks and sank our boat, leaving us swimming in Hong Kong Harbor. Despite our heavy handicap we eventually did really well.

In 1980, Team USA was invited back again to participate in the races held in Hong Kong and also in Singapore. After the long flight across the Pacific from Hawaii, the team checked into a fancy Hong Kong hotel for some much needed sleep.

Early the next day, I decided to jog in the city. I enjoyed running early in the morning thru this foreign city because I got to see the city come alive, observing school kids in matching uniforms waiting for the school bus, shop owners starting their business day, and old folks gathering in parks to practice the ancient art of Tai-Chi.

As I had done the year before, my route for jogging took me right through the city of Hong Kong toward the airport and then back to the hotel, probably not more than a five mile run. Leaving the hotel, I started running down the sidewalk just to loosen up. My slow pace jog started to pick up so I took a fast glance to the left and darted across the street since I didn't see any on-coming traffic.

That was a near fatal mistake. Traffic flow in Hong Kong is opposite from America. Instead of looking to the left, I was supposed to look to the right for oncoming traffic. Now it was too late. I was well into the second lane of the expressway when something told me "Get back. Get out of there!"

I glanced to the right, and heard a tour bus, forty feet away with his air horn blasting and also a lot of traffic that was about to wipe me out. The air horn shocked the movement out of me and I almost froze in my tracks. Instead, I made a desperate jump back to the curbside from the second lane. I don't know how I did it or who carried me, but I made it to the curb just as the traffic and tour bus roared by. My shoes weren't so lucky because they were still in the road being run over. I jumped right out of them.

    Someone was watching over me and carried me that 20 feet back to the curbside in a flash. As I have witnessed from other experiences, that voice was gone as quickly as it came. I got my shoes on again, caught my breath and continued running through Hong Kong. That day I was very, very lucky.

CHAPTER 10

WARNED BUT HELPLESS

You're probably wondering if I ever missed a calling, or declined to act when called on to help. Well there's been times when I wasn't clear on what was happening and in some incidents I wasn't able to react for an assortment of reasons.

Sometimes the situations left me so puzzled I couldn't figure out how I should be involved while at the same time that ever-present voice intensifies dramatically until I finally move into action. Then there were times I couldn't get people to believe me when I told them about a dangerous situation soon to happen, so I would end up frustrated. Sometimes when a message of danger is directed right at me, I ignore it until it was almost too late. That's when I would say, "Something Told Me and I should have listened."

These next four stories are great examples of what happens if I don't get involved or no one wants to believe what I'm trying to tell them. Things go wrong and people end up dead.

In the first story, "A Picnic Tragedy," I'm tired, exhausted and lazy. When I finally got going it was too late, someone died. There was always a lingering question that stayed with me long after the incident. Why me? What was the connection that tried to get me to help that person.

In "Thank God for Traffic," somebody needed help and I couldn't be bothered. I actually tried to ignore what I was hearing. I waited until the last few seconds until I had to jump in to save this person. It was a close call and he could have died if I didn't make a move at the right time.

The next incident, "Sixty Second Warning," was similar in circumstances but a little puzzling because I couldn't figure out how I was supposed to be of help. In the final outcome, two people ended up injured and they were lucky because they could have died.

The last story, "Fire Trap Hotel," turns into a tragedy after I was gone. This was one of those times when I tried to warn others that something serious was going to happen, but nobody took me seriously.

In the second volume of this "Something Told Me series," you'll find two stories that relate to this same subject. No one wanted to believe what I was trying to tell them so I had to let it go, let everything play out, and the consequences were devastating.

CHAPTER 11

Kualoa park with Chinaman's Hat island in Kaneohe Bay.

A PICNIC TRAGEDY

This next story tells of a tragic incident in January of 1982 at Kualoa Beach Park, on the island of Oahu. I had just arrived back in Hawaii for a two-week vacation from my job as an interstate truck driver in Southern California. I was staying at a girlfriend's house and my plan was to stay hidden here for two weeks and not call any friends or family. I wanted to enjoy Anna's company and thaw out from the rough winter I was having on the interstate freeways between the east and west coast.

My last two months on the Interstates had been grueling because of the winter weather. Here's an accounting of what it took for me to get back to Hawaii. It started out seven days ago when I left a Reynolds Aluminum plant in Oswego, New York, bound for Portland, Oregon. Oswego is located way up by Lake Ontario. It wasn't long before I was hammered by a winter blizzard where Interstates 390 and 90 connect just outside of Rochester, New York. Because of the bad winter weather, I had to head south into Pennsylvania and get onto Interstate 80 and then shoot across the nation to Portland. Two days out of New York, I was trapped in another snowstorm in Rawlins while crossing the Rockies in Wyoming. The Highway Patrol made every big truck put their chains on just to get away from the area hardest hit. Twenty-four hours later I left Boise, Idaho, on Interstate 84 and got pounded by another frigid winter storm at 2 a.m. Again I had to put chains on my 18-wheeler just to make it over Cabbage Patch Hill that divides Idaho and Oregon. I'm not sure about the story behind that name but maybe if you lost your brakes on this steep hill, you would probably crash and end up as "cabbage."

Anyway chaining up my 18-wheeler took 2 hours, in a driving blizzard and by now it was four in the morning and *"I wasn't having fun yet."* The best part of this trip was driving along the Columbia River Gorge, one of my favorite rivers to follow as I headed to Portland where I had to drop the loaded trailer of aluminum, then hook up to another loaded trailer full of Snickers candy bars and take it to a Safeway Supermarket in Anaheim, Southern California. I only had 24 hours to make my flight. I had to get from Portland to Safeway in Anaheim, a 16 hour drive, drop off this trailer and park this rig at our base yard a few miles away in Buena Park. From there I had to catch a bus to the L.A. airport. I cut it close and barely made the flight home.

So you can see why I was glad to be back in Hawaii for a little rest and recreation and warm weather. Anna had just left for work and I was lying on the couch watching TV, enjoying my time to relax and not do anything. I was glad to be back in Hawaii. I had my custom Harley Davidson chopper motorcycle out in the garage, which had been sitting there since I left, about two months ago. Eventually I would have to charge the battery and fire up the bike. It was overdue for a wash and polish and it needed my attention; the typical TLC (tender loving care) that most Harleys always require. I promised Anna that we would take the bike out for a spin when she came home.

While lying on the couch an uneasy feeling surrounded me. It was about 8 a.m. and I wasn't even home for 24 hours when way off in the distance, I was being called upon. I ignored the calls. I didn't want to be bothered. I just wanted to be lazy today. But somebody had other plans for me. Then like a big sledgehammer dropping on my head, something told me, *"Go to Kualoa Park. Something is wrong at Kualoa Beach Park."* I tossed and turned trying to ignore what I heard, but the Voice kept persisting.

I rolled over and put the pillow over my ears and tried to hide from this persistent request. An hour later, I 'm still being told to *"Go to Kualoa Beach Park. Hurry!"* I had a bunch of reasons why I didn't want to go because I just wanted to sleep all day so I yelled out, *"I'm off duty, on vacation and out of commission, I'm tired from jet lag, interstate lag, snowstorms and white line fever, call somebody else. Besides, Anna took the car to work so I don't have any wheels except for my Harley."*

The bike had been sitting for two months and the battery was probably dead. I didn't feel like dealing with it at the time 'cause I would have to drag out the charger, remove the battery and put it on a slow charge. Even that wasn't a guarantee that the battery would work. It was too much of a hassle to rush into and I wasn't about to strap on my big boots to try kicking over the crank a bunch of times.

Now, two hours later that same message is pounding in my head so I finally got up and decided to go. It was a nice morning so I rolled the Harley out, cleaned it up, primed the carburetor and tried the ignition. "Varoom," to my surprise the bike started up, the battery didn't need any charging and now I was ready for the rumble. It's a good day when your Harley cranks up on the first try.

Large beautiful green trees surround the route out

there, a mountain range on the left side and the pristine blue waters of Kaneohe Bay on the right. The bike was running okay despite sitting idle for the last two months. It was a gorgeous day and I was glad to be back home even if it was just for two weeks. The familiar Harley rumble was just what I needed to hear as I cracked open the throttle and I couldn't wait till Anna joined me.

On my way, an ambulance came up from the rear with its sirens and lights going crazy so I pulled off to the side and let it pass. About a minute went by and along comes another ambulance, then a fire truck, and then another ambulance and several police cars all in obvious hot pursuit of an emergency and all heading in the same direction.

Now I'm alarmed. Something is happening. I dropped the hammer on the Harley and got right on the back door of the police car. After following them for a few miles I could see their destination and it was the same place I was heading for. All those emergency vehicles were turning into Kualoa Park and I started to get nervous with goose bumps. This park is a favorite for locals and tourists because it offers so much to do and see. It's located at the end of Kaneohe Bay by Chinaman's Hat and it's a great place to camp, go diving, and lay in the sun.

Upon arriving at the park, I saw a lot of emergency vehicles, more ambulances, fire rescue trucks, police cars and rescue boats from the Marine Corps, Coast Guard and our regular fire department emergency units. Up above the helicopters were buzzing the skies. Something is happening, and this is why I was called out here earlier. I walked into the crowd of rescue workers and found out there was a major rescue going on. At the waters edge was a body under a blanket. Emergency crews were busy attending to a lot of people, mostly school kids and a few adults.

What happened was a group of children from Waipahu Intermediate School were on an excursion to Kualoa Park for a picnic and some fun in the sun. Sixty-four eighth graders attempted to cross a stretch of shallow coral reef to Chinaman's Hat, just offshore from the beach. However, the tide was rising and the conditions of the ocean were not good. The current running between the island and the shore was moving at a fast pace and unexpectedly swept everyone out to sea and into deeper waters. So far, the body of one teacher was found. He died trying to rescue the children.

Now I'm feeling bad. Guilty because I had prior warning at least two hours before this incident actually took place and remorse because I didn't react in time. But how could I know this was going to be my responsibility? I was five miles away and had no idea what was going on down at the park today. What was the connection between this school picnic and me? I did not know any of the teachers or students. I'm not sure I would have made a difference if I had shown up when I was first warned about this incident. I will never know what my connection was with this incident and it bothered me for some time. Maybe it's God's way of calling all Angels to an emergency. Then the Angels call on their human partners to help out in any situation that may come up.

It took a few days to forget about this incident and before I knew it my two-week vacation was over and I was heading back to frigid freeways, foul weather gear and living in my semi-truck for another four to six weeks as I ran my coast-to-coast route. I wasn't looking forward to doing it again because winter weather lasted until March.

CHAPTER 12

THANK GOD FOR TRAFFIC
HONOLULU

These next two stories are very similar and deal with that same persistent voice, warning me of immediate danger that's about to happen to someone else. This warning comes on and does not cease until I get involved with the situation. Most times I'm on it, eager to help and participate in any way I can. Sometimes my mind is on something else and I don't want to be bothered with what's going on at that time. Whatever the case may be, the fact remains that I can be called upon to help anyone in the nick of time, but how does this happen?

The year is 1989 and once again I found myself racing against the clock. It was Friday afternoon, traffic was at its peak and I had a flight to catch. The thought of maneuvering through the rush hour traffic made me a little testy. From my condominium, located just outside of Waikiki, a normal drive to the airport was less than 15 minutes, except today it would probably take an hour to cover the 10-mile distance.

From my vantage point in my high-rise condo I could already see the traffic on McCully Avenue starting to pile up. This was the main thoroughfare to the freeway and I was trying to think of an alternate route to get to the airport, but quickly realized that at this time of day, no other route would be better. When I left the parking lot I turned onto McCully Avenue and cars were bumper-to-bumper, all of them headed to the freeway. Glancing down at my watch I noticed it was moving faster than the traffic.

My frustration grew intensely when I caught the light at the intersection of Algaroba and McCully twice. Cars were tangled up and not moving. After the second time of sitting at the same light, I swung my pickup to the left and headed down Algaroba Street. Several blocks later, I made a right turn onto Hauoli Street and thought this might be a good way to get around all the congestion. Wrong. When I got to the next stop sign at King Street, the situation was worse because it's a six lane one way packed with cars, jammed solid and not moving. I needed to get across all six lanes of traffic to make a left turn onto McCully but it didn't take me long to see that trying to slice across six lanes of traffic would not work today. I had no idea that this traffic confusion was setting me up for a deadly situation, and I was meant to be right here.

While at that stop sign, I noticed a woman about 200 feet away coming toward me on my left side. She was pushing a baby carriage and another child was ahead of her riding a tricycle. The little boy on the tricycle was getting further and further ahead of his mother, just cruising along, not paying any attention to his surroundings, as he pedaled his way down the sidewalk. He must have been about five years old and of Asian descent, probably Vietnamese.

Faintly, the Voice that only I can hear in times of danger began telling me, "Stop this boy, he's going to get hit." Over and over the familiar Voice was pounding the message in my head, "Stop him, he's going to get hit!"

At that moment I could not be bothered with this boy's fate. My concentration was on the traffic in front of me. How would I be able to nudge into this street against six lanes of traffic? It seems the more I tried to make my way into the intersection, the worse the traffic became.

Still the familiar Voice was persistent, "Help him. Stop him. He's going to be hit."

The Voice bellowed at me, causing the anxiety of this situation to grow rapidly. The little boy was at least 100 feet away from the intersection. I reasoned that there were at least four doorways between him and the intersection that he might turn into and anyway the mother was there, although some distance behind this little guy. It was her responsibility to watch her child, not mine. That was how I justified my non-action to the voice that was warning me of the boy's impending danger. My concern was solely to make my flight. All the more, the familiar Voice repeated the same message to me, "Help him! Stop him! This boy is going to be hit!"

With everything else going on, I was getting frustrated. The traffic in front of me wasn't moving at all. It seemed like the traffic was at a standstill on purpose. At this point in time, I was more than a little testy. The warning Voice became more urgent and louder. I was frustrated about the traffic and afraid I might miss my flight, I could have cared less about the little boy's predicament. From what I could see, he was still pretty far from the intersection and he did have one alternative; he could keep pedaling his tricycle, turn right at the corner and not cross the street at all.

Eventually the situation turned into a potential hazard. My mind was off the traffic and off the flight, as I watched the little boy. He kept coming closer to me, pedaling his tricycle down the sidewalk. Just then, a city bus came along in the first lane nearest the curb and stopped at the corner to pick up waiting passengers. The little boy kept coming closer as the big city bus cast its overwhelming shadow around him and created a blind spot next to the boy, hiding him from the six lanes of traffic. As the little guy got closer to the corner, I could tell he was going to continue pedaling right into the intersection. He was not going to stop and wait for his Mom. He was moving faster and faster, attempting to get airborne by jumping off the curb with his big wheel tricycle.

The little boy kept peddling. He was still behind the bus and hidden from the rest of the traffic lanes. Suddenly, a car in the second lane prepared to make a right turn in front of the stopped bus. I envisioned the whole scenario, as I sat in my truck and watched the events unfold. The car was going to kill this little guy.

The silent Voice was coming on louder and faster, "Help him! Stop him!"

The car couldn't see the little guy coming because of the bus. With only seconds left, I slammed my gearshift into park, threw open the door of my truck and bolted into the kid's deadly path. It was too late. He had already committed to jumping off that curb with his tricycle. Knowing I might not make it, I made a desperate long, long, long leap in front of the car. At the same moment, the little boy's tricycle went airborne, off the curb. The boy's screams and the snapping and grinding of his tricycle's death rattle was all I could hear. This was followed by the horrified screams of his mother. When the car finally stopped about 30 feet away, the tricycle was wedged under the front end of the car squished like hamburger. The little boy was in my arms and out of harms way, but scared and pretty shaken up. We landed in the gutter, inches away from the passing car. It was a close call for both of us. My elbows were scrapped up and my trousers were torn.

The passengers in the bus were horrified by what they just witnessed. The driver of the bus jumped out to help us off the ground and the elderly couple in the car sat there for a while, numb. Finally, the old man driving the car got out, checked to see if everyone was okay and thanked me over and over. He said all he saw was me dashing across his path as he made his turn. He never saw the little boy at all. The little guy was shaken up, surprised, and frightened as I handed him to his mother who was in hysterics. When I left, the tricycle was still wedged under the car, partly between the engine and front axle. I don't know how they got it out and I wasn't going to stick around to find out. If I didn't intercept that little guy he would have been squished like his tricycle and most likely would not have survived.

When I got back in my truck, there was a surprise for me. All six lanes on King Street were clear of traffic. There wasn't a car in sight and the streets were empty. After looking back on the whole ordeal, the obvious thing to do was to thank God for traffic. I never saw the little boy again.

CHAPTER 13

A SIXTY SECOND WARNING

This incident is similar to the last one except this time I didn't want to make the same mistake again. In the last story I wasn't interested in trying to help the boy until it was almost too late.

Early one Sunday morning, in 1984, I was working at my part-time job as a tour bus driver for Roberts Hawaii. I had just picked up a busload of tourists from the Ala Moana Hotel located on the edge of Waikiki. These tourists were traveling from Singapore and this would be their first day to enjoy the diverse sights of Honolulu.

Two blocks away from the hotel, at the cross streets of Makaloa and Kaheka, the traffic light changed to red causing me to bring the bus to a halt and wait for the light to return to green. At this intersection, there is a bank on one corner and across the street is a high-rise building. On the third corner is another taller building and on the last corner is Honolulu's busiest firehouse, Station 2, home to Engine 2, Ladder 2, and Rescue 1. Within the 60 second waiting period that it takes the light to turn back to green, a bizarre situation took place.

About 200 feet away on my left side, I noticed two young boys coming toward the intersection. One boy, about 9 years old was pushing a shopping cart with a smaller boy, perhaps about 7 years old, riding inside the cart. They were cruising along down the sidewalk and I wondered why these kids were up playing so early in the morning. It was six-thirty, the streets were empty, no cars were moving and nobody was around.

All of a sudden that alarm, that same familiar voice that talks to me in time of danger, is telling me, "Stop the boys, They will be hit. They're going to get hit. Stop the boys. They will be hit. They're going to get hit." Over and over the message is repeated.

Looking all around, there were no cars coming from any direction. It's just my tour bus stopped at this light. This part of town is still asleep because it's so early on a Sunday, yet that voice is asking me to stop these young boys because they are going to be hit. I looked up at the high rise buildings above them, thinking that perhaps something might fall on them, but there wasn't anything happening up there. Still moving slowly toward me, the boys are about 100 feet away and coming closer to the intersection.

What can I do? Am I supposed to jump out of this bus, hold up my hands like a school crossing guard, and tell the boys to wait because they might get hit? They'll think I'm crazy, because there are no moving vehicles around. My light is still red, but will turn green any second now. Finally the older boy pushes the cart up to the curb and stops. The "DON'T WALK" sign is flashing in his face and the younger boy is still in the cart. And again that warning voice is telling me, "Do something. Stop the boys. They're going to get hit." What should I do? They are already stopped.

Suddenly, out of nowhere, from my right side comes a speeding taxi trying to beat the yellow light and attempting to make a left turn in front of me. At the same time, the boy pushing the cart anticipated the light changing and decided to step off the curb. He didn't see the speeding taxi that was about to turn in front of them. The impact was intense and loud. What the passengers and I witnessed in the next second was horrifying and it was too late for me to do anything. The taxi hit the shopping cart sending the little boy flying up and over my tour bus. The older kid was tossed in another direction and the shopping cart was crunched and laying about one hundred feet away.

The tourists were stunned. I jumped out of my seat and rushed to the side of the little boy who had landed next to my bus. Then I checked the other bigger kid. They were hurt badly. Quickly I ran into the fire station and got help as the driver got out of the taxi and started to freak-out. Within a minute, firemen were tending to the two young boys, giving them immediate first aid in the few minutes before the ambulance arrived. The poor taxi driver sat on the curb smoking a cigarette and refused any medical attention.

I felt really bad knowing I had been forewarned about this accident, but failed to do something. But really, what could I have done? How was I to know that the boy pushing the shopping cart was going to step off the curb, at the wrong time? After telling the fire captain exactly how the accident happened, I left the area not knowing the condition of the two boys. The next day the newspapers said the boys were recovering from their injuries and they would survive this ordeal.

This next story had me so frustrated because no one wanted to listen to some concerns I had about the safety of the place. There was nothing I could do and it had a sad ending. Pack a bag and you will need a passport, because we're going to Manila.

CHAPTER 14

FIRE TRAP HOTEL

Back in 1977, my wife and I went away to the Philippines for a short weekend trip to Manila. We had two free passes on Philippine Airlines that we had to use before they expired so we planned this particular weekend for our trip. We packed one bag and took three empty suitcases because we intended to do a lot of shopping and take advantage of the low prices in the Philippines.

It was late at night when we finally arrived and checked into our hotel and we were both exhausted from the long flight. Marlene took a shower and I walked around the hotel looking for its fire escapes and exits just in case of an emergency. This is a habit I started since being trapped in a burning building when I was a teenager. This habit also extends to crowded nightclubs, concert halls, theaters and restaurants that I may be in. I took a short stroll around the 6th floor to locate the exits and memorize each one. It was a very old hotel constructed out of wood, circular in shape with two elevator shafts and the fire escape stairs in the middle of the building. I thought this was a bad design because if you had a fire on the bottom floors, this escape stairs would lead you into the fire.

I looked at the balconies of the rooms and discovered they led nowhere. Another door I found led to a dead-end corridor and other exits were blocked with piles of bed frames, tables and chairs with locked doors leading outside. The place was a total firetrap.

Then it happened. When I opened another door that was supposed to lead to the fire escape steps I heard people yelling and screaming. I instantly felt a sense of panic and claustrophobia. Increasingly, fear grew within me as the screaming and yelling grew louder and people were scrambling in a panic. There was thick smoke filling the halls and I felt the intense heat from the fire. The hotel turned into an inferno. Panic-stricken guests where trying to make it to safety down the fire escape but never had a chance as smoke overcame them. The only way out was down the fire escape in the center of the building.

Closing the door behind me I felt a sense of relief, but I was sweating from head to toe. What did I just go thru? Was it a bad dream? A premonition? A message? I made it back to the room quickly and woke up Marlene.

"Eh, we gotta blow this place. It's a firetrap!"
"Kiks, you're crazy. Come to bed and get some sleep."
"Babe, let's check out now and find another place to stay."
"But Kiks, that would be hard to do. Besides, our room is "comp" and we are only staying here for two nights."

I couldn't get comfortable in this place. The bad feelings about this hotel still bothered me. I went downstairs to the front desk and told them their hotel was a firetrap and asked that we be moved to a lower floor, something on the ground. But nothing was available.

Martial law was in effect back then. No one was allowed on the streets after 11 p.m. If you got caught you could be arrested or even face a firing squad. That ended my idea of going out all night. All I could do was wait until morning when we could get out of the hotel. The trip ended up being up being fun in spite of the restrictions and we did manage to make it through the two nights without any incident. The bad feeling that came over me for those few minutes was only a preview to what was really going to happen. Something was trying to warn me about this hotel being a firetrap and I tried to pass on the warning but it went nowhere fast.

One week later and back in Hawaii, the breaking headline news made me realize my fears were real. The hotel was engulfed in a tragic fire that killed seventy-five people who were trapped inside the burning inferno.

CHAPTER 15

DON'T ASK QUESTIONS

As the years went on I found myself involved in more and more situations to help someone out of trouble and not once did I question why this was happening to me. I just did it. I gained more confidence with every different incident, no matter how deadly it was because I had faith that I would be okay. Luckily, I was still in my twenties and thirties and physically in decent shape to jump into anything that came up. A lot of incidents were those quick ones where I had only one fast message directed at me, a warning with no chance to be repeated. I had to react to it instantly and never asked, "why?" If I didn't listen and didn't react I might end up dead. Usually these messages were meant for me because an unexpected danger was bearing down on me at that moment. Many times it was directed at me, to save someone else from certain death.

There where times when I was "Johnny on the spot," involved in many near drowning situations where I had to react to save someone from a rough ocean, high surf, strong current, a boating mishap, or from a fall into a swimming pool, canal or the harbor. It became second nature and I accepted it every time and asked no questions.

A few times I was sent to avert a suicide about to take place and I was able to talk the person out of their crazy idea and get them to seek outside help. Then there was the time when I got to another person too late, only to find blood, guts and brains splattered on the living room ceiling and walls. It's times like these that made me wonder how I was connected to this situation, because I didn't know the person involved.

Probably the most intense situation to be tossed into is a murder that's going down, and about to happen. On five separate occasions I found myself involved by trying to save someone from a potential murder and sometimes I was on the wrong end of the barrel or knife. It's a gamble to step in and try to save someone, and for me it all comes down to confidence, trust and faith. I've learned a few things when put into a situation where the intention is to save the person in trouble. The element of surprise has to be on your side, you must have a bulletproof plan, react, and don't ask questions. Out of the five potential murder incidents I've been involved in, all the intended victims survived. I chose to write about two of these incidents. The next story is one of them and in the end I'm the one who's nearly killed. The other story will be in the second volume of "Something Told Me."

For the longest time I wondered how and why I was involved in all of this life or death stuff, mostly with strangers and sometimes with friends. It wasn't until I was in my forties when I started asking myself, "Why Me?" This has been going on for years and it's time I found out about this special kind of gift that I've been blessed with. But the more I asked myself, "Why Me?" The answer I got was, "Why not me?" Probably the biggest reason I didn't say anything to anybody was because I didn't know who to ask. If I brought up this subject to anybody say, pre-1990, they would have thought I was a nut case. Since the early nineties more and more people were coming forward to talk about their encounters with a miracle and that's when I started to open up and talk about this.

After holding on to this secret for forty years I met with several pastor friends at different times and places of worship. Our talks went on for days as they sat in amazement listening to what I had to say. In the end they all encouraged me to give testimony in their churches and write a book so others can benefit from my experiences. "Yeah right, me talk in public and write a book, highly unlikely."

By the early 1990's, zillions of articles were being written in magazines and hardcover books. Television screens saw a jump in programs about miracles and life-saving incidents. But in my case, it's different because it's just one person and it keeps happening. I haven't heard or read anything close to what I've been experiencing so I figured if I write about it, maybe more people will come forward to talk about the same thing that I've been going through.

In this next story you'll be facing a Point Blank threat. You're not a policeman, but someone is in serious trouble and needs immediate help. Your chances of calling the police are zero and this person's life depends on your actions. The bad guys are heavily armed and you are outnumbered and have no weapons. This is that point of no return where once you commit there is no turning back because if you fail to save this person, then you probably will be murdered by these thugs. Now would YOU risk your life to save this person? If you're coming with me, then grab a big pipe and watch my back, because I'm jumping in.

CHAPTER 16

POINT BLANK

A great way to see the real beauty of the United States is cruising in a car, motor home, motorcycle or a big semi-truck. So driving my big 18-wheeler and getting paid at the same time was the ideal way for me to see our great nation, especially since I was from Hawaii. I prefer to see the sights from high atop a semi while making my way down a road I've never been on before.

Those purple mountains majesty and golden waves of grain are truly sights to see. America was greatly blessed when God shed his grace on thee.

As for trucking the U.S.A. in my other life, I was a gypsy trucker, living in my semi-truck while zigzagging across the nation and staying at my favorite truck stops along the way. I've been there and done that many times over, through every kind of weather condition that Mother Nature could dish out. I felt right at home running my big truck coast to coast, up and down the eastern seaboard or doing Mexico to Toronto turnarounds with the king of the airwaves, "Wolf Man Jack" booming thru my speakers, keeping me awake and alive. I saw all 48 states while driving over every major interstate and highway in the U.S.A. The funny part was when I did all this and still managed to live in Hawaii. That was a nuts time but I had it set up where I'd spend six weeks running the interstates, then I'd fly home to Hawaii for two weeks for some R&R. After that I'd fly back to Los Angeles, hop in my big rig and do it all over again.

LIFE ON THE ROAD

Hours and days behind the wheel takes a toll on any driver regardless of whether you are a union man, renegade or owner operator. Being a single guy on the open road away from family and friends, pets and your favorite pillow for days at a time is a rough way of life. Sometimes it sucks and other times it's a great escape.

When this story took place I drove for a trucking outfit that was located in Orange County, in Southern California. We hauled brand new wooden pallets to Northern California and Oregon. Our return load was giant timber from the many lumber mills in the Pacific Northwest area. We'd take it back to the pallet company in Southern California where they would cut the timber to 2x4 lumber to make wooden pallets. Other times we would be taking timber to lumberyards in California, Nevada or Arizona.

This particular route had us using the I-5 interstate freeway to shuttle north and south between California and the Pacific Northwest. It was okay because at least I'd be home after four days on the road. It could have been worse. I could have been doing coast to coast turn-arounds and away from home for weeks at a time.

The return leg of this trip started at a lumber mill outside of Portland, Oregon. I was loaded down with timber destined for a lumberyard in Southern California so I spent the night at Jubitz truck stop in Portland and looked at my map book to figure out where I was heading since I had never been to this particular company before.

When looking at the map book, I found two things, one good and one bad. The good thing was the lumber company was close to the freeway so access in and out would be easy. The bad was the location of the company in a high crime district. It didn't take me long to flash back to the riots, shootings, and gang warfare for which this metropolitan area was noted.

I left Jubitz before sunrise but first I loaded up with $25 worth of assorted chocolates to snack on while I drove south. This trip would be close to 970 miles and take about 16 hours of driving time so I would break it up into two legs. The first leg would be around 10 hours, taking me down to a town almost in the middle of California on the I-5 called Santa Nella. I spent the night at a Truck Stop and then left before sun-up the next morning because my destination was just 6 hours away.

After driving for a few hours I stopped for a grilled cheese sandwich and more chocolate at the 76 Truck Stop in Buttonwillow, just off the I-5 and outside of Bakersfield, California. I had wiped out all of my snacks so I needed to get more of the extra large Halloween size bags of Snickers, Hershey Almond Bars, Hershey Kisses and the giant bag of Reese's Peanut Butter Cups. Washing this down with Pepsi or chocalate shakes was how I stayed awake at the wheel. I'm not a coffee person, so my craving for sweets was beyond imagination. I was a sugar addict. It was a great way to keep my six-foot, 180-pound frame nice and slim.

A few more hours of driving went by and I finally found my way to the lumber company. The unloading process went fast, because their giant forklift was able to grab the huge load of timbers in two picks. In fact it took longer to curl up and put away the tie-down straps than it did to unload the rig. The final chore was to bring my logbooks up to date, so I could turn them in when I got back. The logbook is a record of all of your on and off duty driving hours. I kept three of these logbooks, one for the company's records, one to get by the Highway Patrol, and one for illegal switching.

Once the truck was empty, I could focus on getting home in time for dinner. The thought of a hot shower followed by a cold bottle of soda and a fat juicy porterhouse steak sounded like a great way to spend a quiet evening.

WRONG TURNS

Everything began to go wrong when I left the company's parking lot. The first thing I did was turn in the wrong direction. I found myself heading away from the southbound freeway ramp. I was a little angry because all I wanted to do was get on the freeway and head home.

The only thing I could do, after making a wrong turn, was to make another turn and go around the block. I turned on the first street that came up on the right. When I found this street to be very narrow with cars parked illegally on both sides of the road, I realized, with some irritation, that my plan was not working out as easily as I hoped. The rig was close to 60 feet long and trying to worm my way through the maze of tight corners was getting me uptight. Finally getting around all that mess, I came upon another surprise. At the corner leading back to the street I needed, was a big sign saying No Left Turn. Now I was swearing. That meant turning right again and finding another way to the southbound freeway ramp. *At that point I had no way of knowing all these diversions and distractions were setting me up for something very serious, in fact something deadly.*

Again I was going in the wrong direction, and looking for a place to turn around. I saw a road up ahead that looked good and seemed wide enough to get in and out of, so I went for it. It looked like a main street with plenty of room to maneuver the rig. Making my turn, I could see that it wasn't a good place to be. Crime, poverty, and unrest were all very apparent. While traffic was moving slowly down the road, I was able to get a good look at the lifestyles of the not so rich and famous. Lining the streets were bums, young punks and homeless types. The scene was right out of the movies. Graffiti was sprayed on everything, with the exception of a few real works of art. This place had the look of trouble waiting to happen. Traffic was at a crawl because of a light signal up ahead. Eventually, I got up to the light and waited for it to turn green.

While sitting at the light, it started to happen. That familiar Voice I hear only in time of trouble was giving me a message. It wasn't hard to figure out the warning. The Voice came louder and faster. The message was clear and kept repeating itself over and over, "Help her, help her." The Voice comes on like an anxiety attack if I don't react to it. Then it disappears, when I start to respond to its warning. "Help her, help her," kept ringing out. I was looking around and saw nothing happening, no commotion anywhere. What was I supposed to see, was someone in trouble? Still the Voice was persistent. It was asking me to intervene with something I couldn't see. What was I looking for?

Then I saw it, down the road something caught my eye. About a half block away, up on a second floor balcony, a young woman was struggling and screaming her head off. Some men were dragging her down a flight of stairs, and it didn't look good. The Voice kept repeating its message, "Help her." Witnessing the woman's dilemma was enough for me to know that I would get involved. Right on cue and adding fuel to the fire, a gathering angry crowd was cheering her attackers on.

The traffic light was still red as I sat there witnessing this poor lady's predicament. With no time to wait until the light turned green, and no traffic coming, I drove across the intersection and slowly headed down the street to where the action was taking place. My first thought was maybe these guys were plain-clothes cops.

A KIDNAPPING GOING DOWN

As I got closer the problem became more evident to me. It was a kidnapping going down. These guys were not the police. The woman was thrown out onto the sidewalk from a doorway and was followed by three armed men. You could feel her pain as she bounced and rolled down the walkway. With a futile attempt, she tried to get up and run away from her assailants. Again she was slammed to the ground and a knife was placed at her neck causing me to hold my breath. I was infuriated by what I saw and nobody around offered her any help. She looked like she could be an attorney, because she was wearing a nice suit and carrying a large briefcase.

One of her attackers was armed with a pistol, one with a sawed off shotgun and the other was brandishing a nasty blade. They were all pretty husky under their leather jackets. She was helpless. They shoved her into the backseat of a parked car, ready to take off with their new unwilling passenger. I had no idea how I was going to handle this situation myself. There was little time to think about how I would help the lady.

I'm not John Wayne or Charles Bronson, but I have something just like them. Total confidence, no fear, and big balls to step up and do something.

The crowd of onlookers was cheering loudly, but the woman's screams could be heard above it all. I hoped someone was watching the commotion and called the police because I didn't know where to find a phone. I needed to buy some time and figure out how I was going to help her survive this ordeal without getting myself in trouble too.

I parked my rig next to their car, blocking them in so they couldn't leave. Just in case I needed to make a quick escape, I left the engine idling, with only the trailer brake engaged. My initial idea was to act lost and tell them I was looking for a certain street. I started looking around in the cab for a big heavy pipe, a breaker bar that was supposed to be under my seat. I never found it because I stuck it under the passenger seat the last time I used it. I could hear them yelling at me from their car. Sounds of them swearing began to ring out, telling me to move my truck. Louder and louder their screams were directed at me. One of them got out of the car and climbed up the passenger side of my truck.

Leaning inside the open window, he pulled out a 9mm automatic pistol, stretched across the cab and held it about two feet from my head. He began yelling and swearing loudly, then asked, "Que paso, what are you trying to do, be a hero to this gringo?" The idea of acting lost changed instantly. My response to him was way off the wall. I said, "Back off Jack....Que paso your ass, let the lady go." I don't know where that came from, but at that instant the trouble started.

Before he could react, I hit his hand, attempting to knock the gun away. The blow threw him off balance causing him to slide down the outside of the truck. He was yelling something to his buddies, which brought them flying out of their car and in a dash toward my truck. Now I was under siege by the three-armed men. I needed a miracle. Being very calm, my only thought was to protect myself and try to get the woman free. Everything happened so quickly and it was over in sixty seconds.

The guy with the nasty looking blade came running

for the driver's side of the truck. With a well-timed hit and a full force blow, I swung open the driver's side door and slammed him in the face. He fell to the street. At the same time, the first guy managed to climb up the passenger side of my truck again and leaned in the window. He was yelling that I was about to die as he aimed his 9mm pistol a foot away from my face. Meanwhile, the third guy, the one with the sawed-off shotgun, climbed up the front of my rig, lowered the barrel and took aim. He was ready to blast me through the windshield.

I started to struggle with the guy who had the 9mm pistol. I grabbed the gun and wrestled with him while still in the driver's seat. I was looking straight down the wrong end of the barrel as I fought for control of the weapon, when a feeling of total confidence engulfed me. I was very calm as he pulled the trigger at point blank range. The gun jammed. Again he tried pulling the trigger as we wrestled for the gun, and once again, the gun jammed. He was swearing and yelling at the guy with the shotgun to shoot me. In an instant I dumped the gearshift into third and released the trailer brakes. The truck lurched forward throwing the guy with the shotgun off the front of the cab. He managed to scramble away before the big wheels of the semi rolled over him.

As the truck moved ahead, the guy with the pistol was trying to squirm out of the window, but he was temporarily trapped. I managed to hit the power window button located on the console. It made the window rise leaving this guy with no other choice but to bail out. Right about this time, sirens could be heard and the police were arriving from all directions. As I pulled away, my rearview mirror showed me what was left of the incident. The woman got out of the car and was running toward one of the police units. The three men took off sprinting in different directions quickly melting into the crowd.

Leaving the scene was the best option for me. The last thing I needed was for someone to get the name of my employer off the truck doors and try to track me down. I didn't see any reason to stick around and talk to the police. The lady was safe, and I came away alive. It was a close call for both of us. No one got hurt except for the egos of those three guys. The freeway ramp was close by and soon I was headed southbound with the hammer down and my adrenaline was pumping faster than my big truck's wheels.

I never saw the young lady again and never went back into that part of town. The rest of the evening gave me time to reflect on what had happened and how everything took place. It was a classic set up. Surely somebody was watching over her that day, and protected me as well. I gotta say, it was a close call for one trucker this day.

Okay so much for big trucks. Let's go to Maui and have fun and take in some ocean adventure. How about fast boats ripping across an open ocean and catching swells that you can ride for miles? If you're up for this, then take your sea-sick pills or slap on them patches because we're going trolling for some serious action.

CHAPTER 17

SPEED SAILING
It's Happening In Hawaii

Sailing canoe "Eddie Aikau," on a fast smoking ride from Maui to Oahu across Molokai channel.

REVIVING THE SPORT OF SPEED SAILING

Speed Sailing
The Channels between Oahu and Maui

The sport of sailing canoes was popular in Hawaii back around the 1800's and well past the turn of the century. Eventually sailing canoes faded out as a sport in the early 1940's because of World War II. Luckily the efforts of several canoe enthusiasts revived this old form of Hawaiian canoe sailing in 1987 with a race from the island of Oahu to the island of Kauai, a distance of 90 miles across the open ocean.

By 1989, the materials and canoe designs were very high tech. To build a new sailing canoe with the proper

The "Eddie Aikau" with Hokulea's crew enters Kauai's shores after sailing 95 miles from Oahu.

Hokulea crew upon arriving at Nawiliwili Harbor, Kauai with the "Eddie Aikau" canoe. (l to r) Snake Ahee, Clyde Aikau, Kiks, John Kruse, Billy Richards and Kimo Lyman.

equipment for an open ocean channel crossing cost around twelve thousand dollars. The fiberglass hull is 45 feet long, 18 inches wide, and almost two feet at its highest point and has to weigh 400 pounds. Add on a 150 square foot sailing rig, outriggers, spray covers, trampoline and the weight of your sailing canoe could reach 600 pounds. A crew of six and safety equipment for everyone brings the total weight of this water rocket close to 1800 pounds.

Having almost 40 feet of water line under you, coupled with a draft of only eight to ten inches, you are on a high speed sailing sled. Put this together with a nice strong trade wind breeze and a following sea, and you're looking at a ride much better than Disneyland can offer. Catch an open ocean swell on close reach, and it's possible to ride it out for miles at a speed averaging 16 to 24 knots. The experience is incredible, the speed unbelievable. It's possible for a single hull sailing canoe to cross the Molokai channel to the island of Oahu, about 26 miles away, in little less than two hours, if it is a favorable sailing day. Sailing and surfing with the same ocean swell for a long distance, combined with high speed, and a tremendous force of water flying at you, guarantees all this excitement will be hard to forget. "Speed Sailing....It's happening in Hawaii."

Of course, there are dangers. In an instant the sailing canoe can flip over, lines to the mast can snap or water can pour through the spray canvas and swamp your vessel. Each member of the crew has to be able to react to all types of danger with good judgment. The last thing you want to have happen is for your canoe to swamp and go under, especially in an open ocean channel crossing.

Even to attempt such a crossing, another essential must for your sailing canoe is an escort boat. The escort boat has to be a minimum of 22 feet long and must be able to keep up with the demanding speed of 18 knots or better and it has to assist the sailing canoe in any type of situation. In the event the sailing canoe sinks or breaks up, the escort boat must be able to carry all the crew of the sailing canoe without putting itself in danger. The worst-case scenario would be, if your sailing canoe got into trouble and then have your escort boat sink at the same time while trying to save the canoe. If all the safety equipment on both vessels is not readily available, this scenario can easily turn into a nightmare especially in an open ocean crossing.

THE RACE FROM MAUI TO OAHU

On Memorial Day weekend in 1989, the worst case scenario happened and it was almost fatal. This was the first sailing canoe race from Kaanapali Beach, Maui, to Waikiki Beach, Oahu. The course for this 75-mile race includes crossing the four channels that separate the islands of Maui, Lanai, Molokai, and Oahu. The wind directions and current changes are many and the ocean conditions range from glassy to heavy seas. The scenery is spectacular with all the different island backdrops that surround you. The abundance of rainbows, dolphins, whales and the vast array of colors reflecting off the clouds and ocean waves add to this exciting race. Our third and newest sailing canoe, the *Eddie Aikau*, was just completed but not ready for this sailing race. So our next option was to use a brand new 25-foot Larsen speedboat on loan from Windward Boats in Kailua and escort a sailing canoe team back to Oahu. To begin this weekend of fun meant we would have to launch this boat on our home island of Oahu and travel across four open ocean channels to the island of Maui. I had done this crossing many times before and invited a new friend to come along. A talented mechanic, Leif was new to the islands by way of Minnesota.

Lief loaded the boat with the proper safety equipment,

fueled it and early Saturday morning at seven, we left the Hawaii Kai boat ramp located on the eastern tip of Oahu and headed out to Maui. The first channel crossing was 26 miles to the island of Molokai. This is a very moody channel with many different conditions ranging from very calm to down right nasty and ugly and rated as one of the roughest channels in the world.

Mike Kincaid's sailing canoe and the rest of the fleet at the start of the 75 mile Maui to Waikiki Beach race.

The first leg of our trip was done in 45 minutes because the ocean conditions were flat and glassy. Our first stop on the island of Molokai was at Hale O Lono harbor, an abandoned sandpit quarry on the southwest side of the island. Our next stop was 14 miles down the coast at the main town of Kaunakakai, on the island of Molokai. We rested here for an hour filling up on sandwiches, cookies and cold drinks for breakfast. Molokai is known as the friendly island and is my favorite place to visit and kick back. The locals here in Hawaii call it God's country. We left and moved swiftly with a wide-open throttle down to the south coast of Molokai, and crossed the glassy and flat channel to Maui. By 11 a.m. we were tied up in Lahaina, Maui. We did the 65-mile crossing from Oahu in four hours, thanks to perfect ocean conditions. We eventually made our way into Lahaina town that afternoon to take on food, water and whatever else we needed for the trip back to Oahu. After dinner and a night in Lahaina, we headed back to the pier where Leif got involved in an all night poker game on another escort boat. I hit the sack early as exhaustion had finally caught up with me.

The next morning we checked in with the officials and waited for this drag race at sea. We would be escorting Mike Kincaid, one of the pioneers who revived the sport of sailing canoe races and the President of the Hawaiian Canoe Sailing Association. As the race got closer to starting, we decided to leave the pack of escort boats and scan the starting line just to see each sailing canoe and then headed out into the channel to wait for the race to start. By checking all the canoes and sailing rigs, we were able to remember most of the different colored sails which made it easier to identify each sailing canoe from a distance. It was a great day for racing inter-island, and another beautiful Maui morning with its mountains, valleys and ocean blending into a picture perfect Kodak moment. The beauty of our islands never ceases to amaze me.

We were at least one mile ahead of the sailing canoes when the race started and it would be a few minutes before all the sailing canoes would break away from the pack to choose their best course for Waikiki Beach, seven hours away. We spotted our sailing canoe not too far away and it would be a couple of minutes before they caught up to us. We finally came together a mile into the race, and they were smoking, doing better that 20 knots, with a strong trade wind breeze that funnels down the slot between the islands of Molokai and Maui. Ocean spray was blasting the back half of this fast moving canoe making it hard to see the last two guys who were in charge of steering this high-speed water sled. Our escort boat was flying just trying to stay with these guys. The demanding speed required total concentration because we were airborne a lot, just jumping over waves and swells. What a rush! What excitement! Handling a fast moving boat through the maze of large ocean swells is like riding a dirt bike on rough terrain filled with jumps and ditches. It quickly takes a toll on your body

Jimmy Kincaid, far left, in the sailing canoe "Ikaika," at the start of the race.

JIMMY'S IN TROUBLE

We were along side Mike's sailing canoe for about twenty minutes when a strange thing happened. That Voice that warns me of danger was back, and it was telling me something. Over and over it kept saying the same thing very softly, but very direct. "Jimmy's in trouble. Jimmy needs help." This went on for 10 minutes. The Voice sounded familiar, but I couldn't place it. It was the Voice of someone I knew, a female Voice. Who is it I wondered? We maneuvered over to Mike's sailing canoe and told him we were going to leave for a while to check on Jimmy and we would be back soon. Leif was puzzled. "Hey, why are we turning back?" "I think Jimmy's in trouble."

Mike and Jimmy are brothers. Jimmy had his own sailing canoe team and he was a veteran of several channel crossings. We remembered what his sail looked like but could not find him as we headed past all the other sailing canoes on our way back to Maui. We were entering the area where the two channels crossed and the ocean was kicking up as we traveled a good distance, and there was no sight of Jimmy. That same persistent familiar voice was back again, "Jimmy's in trouble." As soon as we passed all the sailing canoes I sensed something was wrong because he was not in the pack of sailing canoes that passed by. We headed in a southeasterly direction for a few more minutes and finally, way off in the distance we could see the sail of Jimmy's canoe fluttering in the wind, a clear sign that the canoe was not making any headway and probably had stopped for a minor change or repair. By now we were one mile away from him and moving quickly with our throttle full ahead.

The ocean was kicking up to about four feet with white caps and we figured we could assist them so they could get back into the race again. As we got closer, we were able to see the trouble. Jimmy's canoe had taken on a lot of water, which was pouring in faster than the crew could bail it out. Jimmy was hurrying around the canoe trying to do everything he could to stop it from sinking. It was too late. The canoe sank leaving his crew in the water hanging onto their submerged canoe. The throttle to our 125 horsepower Johnson was wide open and we were still about a minute away from them.

When we pulled up the situation turned bad. The worse case scenario happened. Their escort boat, a 22-foot open deck center console, with twin 125 horsepower Johnson motors was in trouble because the stern of their boat was facing oncoming ocean swells. One wave went over the transom and filled up the rear of the open-deck boat. Immediately, the next wave poured into the boat. Spilling in more unwanted water, it knocked out one of the two engines. In ten seconds their escort boat rolled over on it's left side, filled up with water and sank. Their desperately needed emergency gear went down with the boat and they had no way to call for help. We couldn't believe what we had just witnessed as we arrived on the scene. There were four people, two men and two teenage boys on board when the boat rolled over and sank.

The two boys and one adult surfaced and the other person was missing and didn't surface. Someone yelled that it was B.S. and his legs were tangled in the rope that pulled him under. We spotted him underwater struggling from the ropes that had him trapped. He was in a panic when we dove in and pulled him up and were able to get him to the surface in the nick of time. Overcome with shock and exhaustion, he was seconds from drowning. They were lucky we arrived on the scene in time to be of help.

After gathering the crewmen from the canoe and the escort boat we started sending out May Day signals in hopes that we could reach the official safety boats that were out there somewhere. We needed a big boat to get all these guys and their submerged canoe back to land. Finally two hours later a bigger boat showed up and when everyone was safely aboard the big boat, Leif and I started back into the channel to catch up with Mike Kincaid's canoe. Two hours passed while we were helping with this rescue. We were heading back looking for Mike and his crew, when Leif asked me how I knew Jimmy was going to be in trouble. I just said, *"Something Told Me."*

Jimmy's crew was very grateful we showed up on

the scene just in time to help them, especially B.S. who was caught in the ropes. He couldn't thank me enough. As it turned out, four sailing canoes were forced out of this race, all in this same area of the channel, each ended up being towed by their escort boats to Molokai. The lucky thing about the whole episode was the fact that I was told Jimmy needed help at least 20 minutes before it actually took place. This gave us a chance to get a jump on the situation so we could get to them in time.

We entered the Molokai Channel after running our engines wide open for 30 miles and we finally caught up with Mike and his crew. His crew was doing all right and making good time by catching ocean swells and utilizing their 150 square foot sail to push the sailing canoe along. Off in the distance was the island of Oahu, and the finish line at Waikiki was less than an hour away. We could see the Leeward Kai sailing canoe gaining on us. It was setting up to be a nice race to the finish for the two sailing clubs.

The race from Maui to Waikiki ended with Hui Nalu Canoe Club winning the first place cash prize. It was a long weekend for all involved, especially for Leif and I. We couldn't wait to get to shore and celebrate with all the other crews.

Later that evening after I got home, I called Jimmy's house to see if everything turned out okay. When Jimmy's wife Arte answered the phone, I had a chilling surprise when I heard her Voice. This was the answer to that question that had been bugging me all day. It was Arte's voice that I heard; it was Arte's voice telling me that Jimmy was in trouble.

She was excited and happy to hear from me and started to thank me for helping her husband and crew out of a bad situation. The whole crew was at the house at that moment, filling her in on the day's events. We spoke for a while, then she was able to calm down a little to tell me something else.

Earlier that morning, while at home in Kailua, she had a terrible feeling that something was going to go wrong in this race. So she said a prayer and asked for help and protection for Jimmy and the rest of the crew. She said her prayers were answered because I was able to help them and now they were all at home tonight safe and sound.

She wondered how I knew they were in trouble and how I found them in that big ocean? Without going into detail I just told her, "Something Told Me Jimmy was in trouble and I went looking for him." It really was the power of prayer that worked today for Arte because I picked up on it even though my position out at sea was at least fifty miles away from her home in Kailua. One thing was for sure, it definitely was Arte's voice I heard that morning.

Arte was my good friend and was loved by everyone. She raised two wonderful teenagers and her large circle of girl-friends were special ladies who loved her dearly and were always there to lift her spirits. In 1992, at the young age of forty-one, her long battle with cancer ended and our friend Arte went home to be with her Angels and God.

Aloha Arte

JIMMY'S STORY

This incident happened in 1989, and I can remember it clearly, like it was yesterday. It was the big sailing canoe race. Memorial weekend, and it was a 75-mile course from the island of Maui to Waikiki Beach, on Oahu. Safety is always a big factor when planning an ocean crossing in these sailing canoes. In a racing situation, things are happening at a very fast pace. The slightest miscalculation on wind and swells can cause your team to fall back, and your opponents will have an edge on you. An oversight on the safety precautions while racing can shut you down, and sometimes it can be a very expensive mistake, and it can be fatal too.

This particular race was a bad one for us, because whatever could go wrong did. Things were happening so fast, we barely had time to breathe and it was all over. The sailing canoe got into trouble first and went under. Within a few minutes, our escort boat got in trouble and sank in 10 seconds. We were in a grave situation. One man was tangled in some ropes and went under as the boat sank. I had no way of calling for help because our safety gear and radios went down with the boats. My sail was still up, and was visible for miles but no one knew we were in trouble. In a matter of minutes our two boats were underwater and we were in the middle of the ocean, somewhere between the islands of Molokai, Maui and Lanai.

When I looked up, Kiks was right there in front of us. He was able to find our drowning crewman and rescue him in the last moments of his life. He picked up the two youngest members out of the ocean, my 16-year-old son and a friend from school, then called for assistance and stayed with us until a bigger boat could come to get us. We were lucky because this area is known for those big sharks that are lurking beneath the surface. It was a good thing for the whole crew that he showed up in time to help us. And I didn't know how he knew of our predicament until he told me 10 years later. Many thanks to my friend and that special gift he is blessed with.

James K. Kincaid
Kailua, Hawaii 1999

CHAPTER 18

My first truck when I started Semi-Pro Express in 1978.

Explaining to mom why she can't drive the truck. Loaded on the flatbed are Monier Roofing tiles with a towaable forklift hitched to the back of the trailer. Total length from front to back was 75feet long.

TRUST IN FAITH

Out of all my brushes with death and fatal situations that I've faced, this next story is the second scariest incident that I've been involved with because it took along time to play out and unfold. If you're coming with me on this next one, buckle up tight.

There are a lot of times when a warning is directed to me for the sake of my own safety. In many cases, the Voice is telling me something again and again because I am not taking the message seriously. My next story is a good example of this because I didn't act upon the warnings and I found myself facing a life and death situation. By not listening and not sensing the imminent danger, I had to deal with the consequences. What happens when I don't listen to the warnings? Does my guardian Angel disappear and forget about me? No. Angels do not say, "I told you so" or "You should have listened." Angels never give up but will stay with you through any situation as in this story about a true Trust in Faith. I was able to stay calm and not panic and I put all my faith in the Voice that talked me through the whole ordeal.

Back in the late 1970's, construction was booming and work was plentiful in Hawaii. With the majority of Hawaii's population residing on the island of Oahu, Hawaii's capital city of Honolulu was growing rapidly. New homes were being built at a very fast rate during this construction boom.

Housing developments with hundreds of homes in each new community were sprouting up everywhere. Waikiki, the tourist mecca, was fast becoming a concrete jungle with multiple high-rises shooting skyward. Progress and development were pumping in the islands and construction was endless.

Construction was still cranking in 1978 and I was employed by IML Freight, *(Interstate Mountain Lines)*, a large, trucking outfit from Salt Lake City, Utah. For years this company was amongst the top ten big trucking conglomerates across the United States for freight hauling and interstate trucking. I was the senior driver in the heavy haul division at the Hawaii Terminal for IML. Hauling construction material and giant machinery for construction companies in Hawaii was a daily routine for our division. Around this time rumors were flying that IML might be going out of business and all of the trucks, trailers, and forklifts might be sold off. Weeks later, it was reality. Word from the head office got back to our terminal in Hawaii to get ready to sell everything and close down our terminal. With keen business insight and a gamble, I saw an opportunity to do my own thing, to start my own business. I was 28 years old and having my own business was always a dream for me.

The following week all the equipment went up for sale. I knew which trucks and trailers I wanted and through a leasing plan I took possession of two big semi-trucks, two forty foot flatbed trailers and a big tow-able forklift, all with no money down, my signature, and a promise to pay $500 a month toward the lease. I was very fortunate to capitalize on this chance to step into bigger shoes. In October of 1978, I started Semi-Pro Express. Worried about my decision, my wife, Marlene questioned whether I was doing the right thing.

On that same day of signing the lease, I landed two accounts that IML had to let go. One was with a big construction outfit and the other was a contract with Monier Tile, a company from Australia with the best quality product for roofing. This cement-roofing tile was in high demand and the factory at Campbell Park, on the island of Oahu could not pump out roofing tiles fast enough. Even with three shifts working around the clock, the imbalance between supply and demand was bizarre. Monier tiles were a hot item because it was fire proof, rot proof, termite proof and came in an assortment of colors.

My contract provided all the trucking needs for Monier Tile, from its Campbell Park location on the southwestern tip of the island to every job site on Oahu. The trucks ran 16 hours a day, six days a week and were shut down one day a week for maintenance. Besides running day and night on Oahu, we delivered loads daily to Honolulu Harbor, for shipment by barge to the neighbor islands. In my first 30 days of business, my profits after expenses were BIG $$$. Now Marlene had a different attitude toward the trucking business. Soon the paychecks would get bigger and bigger every 30 days.

SETTING THE SCENE...

Almost fifty percent of Oahu, the third largest island in the Hawaiian chain, is mountainous with jagged cliffs, rolling slopes and deep valleys. Separating Honolulu from the windward side of the island is a large and long mountain range known as the Koolaus. On the town side, these mountains flow into gentle sloping hills and valleys On the windward side, the Koolaus are sheer cliffs, a few peaks as high as 2,000 feet. With cliffs rising straight up into the clouds, the mountains are an awesome sight to behold. These cliffs as well as the sea cliffs on the islands of Molokai and Kauai are the most spectacular of all in the Pacific.

To get to the windward side of the island, three sets of tunnels run through the Koolau Mountain Range. The windward side of Oahu is probably one of the most scenic areas in the whole state of Hawaii. With its towering cliffs and a protected bay, a truly picturesque view welcomes you every time you exit one of the tunnels. It's said that your attitude mellows out and the climate is cooler when you come to the windward side.

Built first in 1959, the Pali Tunnels connect Honolulu to Kailua. The next tunnel, completed in 1965, was the Wilson Tunnel running between Honolulu and Kaneohe. Both the Pali and Wilson Tunnels contributed to the rapid development and population growth on the windward side from the 1960s and into the 1990s. The H-3 Freeway and tunnels opened in 1997. This new H-3 artery speeds the land connection between the military bases of Hickam Air Force Base, Pearl Harbor Naval Shipyard, and Kaneohe Marine Corps Base and also provides residents with faster links from windward Oahu to central and leeward communities.

From Honolulu to the town of Kailua, the easiest and fastest route is up the Pali Highway, a six-mile stretch that passes up through Nuuanu Valley and crosses the Koolau Mountain Range via the Pali Tunnels. Exiting the two short tunnels at an elevation of 1,100 feet, the windward coastline spreads out below you, a picture postcard panoramic view of the tropical Kailua cityscape with the hazel blue-green of the ocean blending into the sky at the horizon. If one desires a better shot of this beautiful scene, the Pali Lookout offers the best location.

A popular tourist stop, the lookout is located just above the tunnels high atop the Koolaus. Watch out though, the occasional winds whistling over the lookout can be playfully exciting, causing hair, bags, dresses and jackets to fly parallel to the ground.

In an automobile, the Pali Highway is a pretty mellow drive as it winds its way through steep cliffs and lush green valleys. In a loaded semi-truck, it's a different story. The semi driver has to be a bit more cautious when descending this part of the highway. With the momentum of the vehicle's weight pushing you down the hill, it becomes a challenge for even the most experienced driver to maintain safe control of a big rig with a heavy load. Of course one of the greatest safety measures for a huge semi-truck is a good set of brakes to ensure safe passage down any hill. Another feature, if your big truck or "rig" is equipped with it, is an engine brake, better known as a "Jacob's brake." An electric switch activates this type of brake. You can leave it on and any time your foot is removed from the accelerator pedal, the "Jake brake" kicks in, chokes the engine, slows it down, and simultaneously drops the speed of the vehicle.

Another way to slow down the vehicle is to drop to lower gears, also known as downshifting. This can only be accomplished if the rpm's (rotations per minute) of the engine are slowing down along with your road speed. So good brakes on the truck and trailer, a strong Jake brake and good timing on the downshifting will almost ensure you of a safe journey down any hill. You've probably heard the loud rumbling sound coming from the mufflers of a big truck or bus just before it comes to a stop, or when its coming down a hill. That sound is from the engine brake being activated to aid in bringing the vehicle to a safe stop.

AND NOW THE STORY...

Now let's fast-forward this story ahead from 1978 to

1980. The business was going great and I was able to expand by adding three employees, a lady friend who handled the bookkeeping and paperwork, and one full-time and one part-time driver. As head honcho, my duties were everything else whenever it was needed from operations manager, to driver, mechanic, janitor and truck washer.

My basic schedule was work, work, and work. The roofing business was great for Monier Tile and my trucking company. Construction in the islands was skyrocketing so my trucking business was doing big time profits. A kid at heart, I was also able to expand my fleet of toys. The custom GMC pickup and a Datsun 280Z were in the garage, the boats were in the driveway and the Harley Davidson was in the master bedroom.

On the morning when this story begins, the trucking jobs started at 5:00 a.m. and I was doing the driving. I pulled two 28' flatbed trailer loads of roofing tile to Brigham Young University, a small college in Laie on Oahu's north shore. Then I went back to Campbell Park to get the next loaded trailer, a 40' flatbed trailer loaded with roofing tile bound for a job site in the Enchanted Lakes area of Kailua. A big housing project was developing there and we were on this particular run for several months. This job meant that I would have to hook up our big tow-able forklift to the back of the semi-trailer and tow it to the job site so I could off load the pallets of tile.

During the last two weeks, everything had fallen out of sync for me and a lot of stuff got put aside, including maintenance on the trucks because Marlene and I were heading for a split-up. At this same time, that little Voice was making its occasional guest appearance, saying to me, "Check your brakes Kii. Check your brakes." I knew it had been some time since I adjusted the brakes on my rig, truck 104. I kept putting it off. I figured I'd slide in all the maintenance over the weekend doing both trucks and trailers at the same time. Still the Voice kept persisting "Check your brakes. Check your brakes."

It was about 12:30 p.m. and lunch was over and the rig was loaded with the forklift connected behind. The trip generally takes an hour, depending on traffic and road construction. The route I planned to take goes directly into Honolulu. It connects to the Pali Highway through Nuuanu Valley. Having done the trip hundreds of times, I thought this one would be another routine delivery. Truck 104 was a three-axle International cab-over with a long frame. Cab-over means a type of truck where the cab sits over the engine. The transmission has 13 forward gears, and the Cummins Diesel has 350 horsepower stuffed in the engine, plus a turbo for that extra kick. But truck 104 was NOT equipped with a Jacob's Brake. No big deal, this was something I didn't miss.

If you were good, you wouldn't need an engine brake anyway. Back then engine brakes were a luxury. In the trucking world, not having a Jake Brake separated the men from the young boys who thought they were "Johnny Truck Drivers."

As the story goes, I passed through Honolulu and began climbing the Pali Highway. I had about six miles to go before I reached the top of the mountain. This took awhile because of the heavy load I was pulling, sixteen pallets of tile weighing a total of 48,000 pounds with the big forklift adding another 14,000 pounds. The truck alone weighed 16,000 pounds and the 40-foot trailer added another 10,000 pounds. Adding all this all up it came to 44 tons, quite a heavy load to pull over the mountain. The total overall length from the front of the truck to the rear of the forklift was 75 feet. You can imagine how tricky it would be to bring something this heavy down a steep grade.

When I reached the top of Nuuanu Valley, I passed through the dense lush green rainforest reserve where tall trees surround both sides of the highway. It kind of looks like the Pacific Northwest, or what you might find in Michigan or even Pennsylvania. About a mile before entering the tunnels, the cliffs of the Koolau Mountains rise high, appearing to be reaching up to the clouds. On rainy days, countless shimmering waterfalls cascade down these cliffs and flow into the reservoir. More awesome is watching these waterfalls on a windy day. The water drops a couple of hundred feet down the cliff, then magically the updraft wind catches the water and blows it back up the mountainside. Upside down waterfalls, Yup. It's even more exciting when five or six of them are going off at the same time, all upside down, it's wild.

As the highway started to descend, it was time to slow the rig by downshifting to a lower gear. From ninth direct gear, I dropped down two gears into seventh direct. The tunnels were just up ahead and my speed was a little too fast, so immediately I moved down another gear to sixth direct. With my road speed down to about 20 mph, this seemed okay. I entered the first tunnel and a fast glance at my watch told me it was almost 1:30 p.m. Traffic was light and cars were flying past me because I was going so slowly. From the sound of the engine, I could tell the engine speed was starting to climb, so I tapped lightly on the brakes, and it seemed to do the trick. Entering the second tunnel, I sense that my speed is still a little slow, but I decide to stay at this speed so I can take a slow cruise down the hill, and enjoy the views from high atop my semi. It was another beautiful day in paradise. Almost out of the second tunnel, I needed another light tap on the brakes to slow the engine speed down, and that's when something happened...NOTHING HAPPENED!

The brake pedal went to the floor. Experiencing the most indescribable feeling that I can't even begin to explain, my heart was in my throat and I was terror-struck. Jolting back to reality, I tried the brake pedal again, and also pulled the emergency brake knob. NOTHING HAPPENED, just squealing noise. "Oh shit," was the only thing I remembered saying and my mind began racing full speed ahead. I knew this wasn't the time to panic. My road speed was picking up. Looking down at the speedometer it indicated 30 mph. If I were just an employee driving for this company, I would have immediately run this rig right into the side barrier just to stop it before I gained any more speed. But since I owned the company, thinking about doing that became a bad idea. At this point, I reached down and tightened my seat belt all the time thinking, "This couldn't be happening to me, if this is a bad dream, I'm ready to wake up now."

The engine started to get louder and my speed kept climbing. I knew not to try down shifting again because it wouldn't go. With the engine winding out the way it was, there was no way I was able to go into another lower gear. If I tried, I'd be trapped in neutral making the truck totally out-of-control. The next stretch of road was critical. The highway level drops even more and in a mile and a half, a tight hairpin turn awaited me. Nowadays there is a runaway truck ramp one mile down from the tunnel. But back in 1980, this particular ramp wasn't built yet. My speed was up to 40 mph and climbing. In another minute I'd be at that hairpin turn.

Right at this time I was ready to kiss my ass goodbye. I prepared myself for death, as I knew making the hairpin turn would be a miracle. The speed limit for this turn is 35 mph. Looking down, the speedometer was up to 55 mph. At this point, I made up my mind about something else too. If there was anybody in my way that could be put in danger, then without hesitation I was going to take this rig off the mountain. A thousand thoughts were flying through my head. "What if I hit somebody? If I'm going to die who's going to pay for the clean up and the damages?" Then I had a crazy but realistic thought. If I drove this rig off the road at the hairpin turn, the valley down below was so deep, nobody would want to clean up the mess and haul this truck back up the mountain, so there would be no mess to clean up and no damages to pay for. Mentally I was ready to die, but there was no time to be scared. I started to say a prayer, when suddenly in the back of my confused mind, I heard that familiar Voice rising above all the chaos racing through my head, "You'll be okay, trust me."

Setting up for this killer turn, I took a fast glance and noted that my speed was now up to 65 mph. The rig was screaming. I was hanging on to this long left hand turn, a complete 180-degree turn. At this speed it would be nuts if you tried this in an automobile, but in a loaded semi . . . it's suicide. My hands were sweating on the wheel; I knew the truck was going to flip over. On the verge of panic, I picked up the hot line and prayed, "Oh God, I need help!"

The truck leaned to the right and I expected it to roll over. Guardrails made of skinny cement posts connected with white wooden planks flew past me like a little picket fence. There was still a ways to go before I could get out of this turn. All the tires were squealing. There was a serious tension on the steering wheel. I was thinking, "There's no way to survive this." Almost instantly, something happened. A calm feeling came over me as I sensed somebody else had their hands on the big steering wheel. Someone was there with me, guiding this run away truck through the turn. Halfway into the turn, I could finally reach up and hang onto the air horn. For the first time I was able to look in my mirrors. I saw a red sports car flying past me. My air horn was loud, blasting its warning to everyone that this truck was in trouble. With the hairpin turn almost over, I couldn't believe it, I made it and I was still rolling. I was able to breathe again.

At this point, the highway straightens out and drops even more. Up ahead is a runaway truck ramp, maybe a half-mile down the hill. Should I or shouldn't I? With a fast glance at the dash I saw my speed was now 70 mph. My mind was racing. "Think, Think." If I go for the ramp, my chances of survival are zero because runaway truck ramps are designed to stop a truck at any cost to the driver. A lot depends on the type of truck it is. In my case, the flat bed trailer behind me was a loaded weapon because of the heavy pallets of roofing tile on it. With the sudden stop caused by the ramp, all the pallets would slide forward off the trailer, and the 48,000 pounds would crush the cab, killing me instantly. If somehow I didn't die, then surely I'd be paralyzed. In all my years on the road, I've seen this happen a few times.

Was I ready for that? Was I ready to die on a run away truck ramp? Hell no. I'll choose my own death. I could see the Grim Reaper waiting at the top of that ramp. The Devil of Death was trying to pull me onto that ramp.

Like I said, runaway truck ramps are designed to stop a truck at any cost, including killing the driver and this particular truck ramp probably is the most poorly designed ramp in the state and across the nation. Because of its poor design, a driver has to hit a certain mark on the ramp to make a safe entry. If a driver misses the mark the truck will flip over as it enters the ramp. I made up my mind to ride out this mountain and hope for the best. The fact that I just made it through the toughest part of this highway convinced me to hang in there. As I passed by the entrance for the ramp, I prayed I was making the right decision.

The engine was screaming, the noise almost unbearable,

and now at 80-mph I was committed because my last chance of hope had just passed. Down the hill a quarter mile ahead is another turn, this time to the right. Just after that turn is an intersection with a blinking yellow light a hundred yards before the bend to warn you if the light at the intersection is red. As luck would have it, the yellow light started to flash and I couldn't see around the bend. How many cars are stopped there, what about the cross traffic?

The truck was going 85 mph now. I was prepared to die if that was the only way to keep from killing some innocent person. Blasting the air horn as I came near the Castle Junction intersection, my speed was picking up and the bend in the highway was fast approaching. Silently I said a prayer, "Oh God, how many cars are in that intersection? Help me please, let the area be clear." The blinking yellow light told me that cars were still stopped at the light and there probably was cross traffic coming onto the highway. Knowing this intersection, I realized that there was no escape if a lot of cars were stopped and that I may have to "flip" this rig and surely die.

I crossed over to the left lane and the rig swerved drastically. Looking down, the speedometer was stuck at 85 mph. I knew I was going faster than that. Now I could see the intersection up ahead. Two cars were in the left turn lanes, three cars were in the middle lane, and that red sports car was in the right lane. To the right of the red car is the shoulder of the road, a ten-foot gap between the car and the traffic light pole. That's my opening as long as the red car stays where he is. I slid back into the right lane, lined myself up for that 10-foot gap and with one hand hanging onto the air horn, Whoosh, I made it through that little gap. No cross traffic was coming. What luck, not even the light pole got hit. The guy in the little red sports car never moved. I wonder what his thoughts were when he saw the giant semi roaring past him just inches away.

Still one problem, the highway did have a few cars ahead of me from the cross traffic that had entered the highway. I wondered, "Will I catch up to them? Will I really have to go off this mountain?" This part of the highway is flat for about a quarter mile after the intersection. The road drops "big time" as it makes a right bend. I knew I was going faster than 85 mph. "No use looking down at the speedometer anymore, it's broken. How long will this transmission hold me in sixth gear before it blows?"

At this point, the highway begins to drop and the steepest part of the mountain is up ahead. With the total weight of the semi rolling down this steep section of highway, I was in for a wild ride. If I survived, it would be a miracle. If it looked like I was going to hit cars, I'd have to take the truck off the ridge. There are about four open areas on the right side of this highway to do this, if that's the only alternative. Still the Angel was with me, calming me, telling me, "You will be okay. Don't worry." I tried to trust what I heard, but at the same time what I saw looked deadly.

I reached the top point before the steep descent. About a half mile down was another intersection fronting the entrance to the Kailua Drive-in Theater. Those cars were still up ahead. My mind raced, "What if that light turns red? Will they hear my air horn? Will they see me coming? Think, Think." The speed increased. The engine was winding out something awful now and the transmission was screaming an unbearable sound. The engine was racing over "max".

The engines are designed to run at a top speed of 2200 rpm. Because of the speed I gained coming down the mountain, the engine was winding out to an incredible 4,000 rpms, way beyond its manufactured design. This means the engine could blow any second. Because the engine sits right under the driver, the pistons would be like torpedoes blasting through the cab of the truck, killing the driver instantly. This is the one time I wished the truck had a scatter shield. A scatter shield is designed to cover engine parts on dragsters and hotrods to protect the driver from engine blowouts.

With everything going through my mind, I decided to go into neutral. With all my trust and faith in the Angel who was talking to me, I stepped down on the clutch to ease up the heavy torque on the transmission, and tried to yank the stick out of sixth gear and into neutral. It was stuck and locked in gear because of the torque and speed of the engine and transmission. But keeping the clutch in kept the truck in a neutral position and the loud sound from the transmission was gone. This seemed to be suicide because now the speed was picking up fast, but the sound of the transmission did not have to be tolerated any longer. The steepest part of the highway was under me now and I was traveling well over 100 mph. No time to be scared. I had to concentrate and stay calm.

Suddenly something happened again. Somebody else had control of the rig on this steep section of highway. I was still in the driver's seat, but I wasn't driving. Someone else was controlling my runaway semi and I could feel myself easing into the state of calm. I was closing in on the three cars ahead of me, but they all had their left blinkers on. They were moving over to the left side of the road. Now the highway was wide open. Taking a quick glance to the right side, I thought I saw that Grim Reaper glaring at me as I flew past him. Because I was not in control of the truck, I was able to glance in my mirrors and see that the forklift was okay and the load still intact.

The intersection was coming up now, with no cars around. As I headed straight down the hill, my speed was well over 100 mph. The vibration was intense. At this point, I was wishing I had installed an engine brake on this rig. I sensed the speed, the rush, and the intensity of this deadly situation. While still calm, I pondered over my next move, "What should I do when I get to the Castle Hospital intersection? Go straight into Kailua or turn right where the road rises and goes toward Waimanalo? As I reached the bottom of the last hill, I sensed that I had regained control of the truck again. The highway is flat for now as I passed the intersection for the road entering Maunawili. My speed was still over 100 mph. Up ahead the road swings to the left and rises. This was a welcoming sight for me because this meant the truck would slow down.

Everything seemed quiet since clutching to neutral. The transmission was not screaming anymore. The engine quieted down along with the rpm's. A new sound was emerging. I heard the familiar rattle of the forklift behind me and the humming of the 18-wheeler tires racing on the pavement. The road started to rise. My speed was dropping and I set up to shift to the highest gear, 13 over-drive. As I climbed the hill, my speed was still fast. Up ahead was Castle Hospital junction, a big intersection. I made the obvious choice to turn right toward Waimanalo.

With the incline slowing the rig down, the right turn was coming up fast. Still stepping on the clutch, I slowly slipped the shift lever into "13th over" and it caught, a fast click down to 13th Direct, and the truck slowed under my control. Another drop in gear and I repeated the same sequence in 12th Gear. I needed to slow the rig down to make the turn. Moving backward through the gears and downshifting to 10th Gear I made it around the corner. The road rises and I began to look for an area to bring the truck over to the side. Just past the residential area, I saw a nice grassy pasture area, a safe place to stop. Today this grassy pasture is home to the Olomana Fire Station.

After pulling over well off the road, I sat in the truck hunched over the wheel with the engine idling. I couldn't believe what had happened in the last five minutes. Catching my breath and gathering my thoughts, I said a small prayer of thanks. Unbuckling my seat belt, I climbed out of the cab and walked slowly toward the back of the trailer. All 18 tires were smoking; even the four big tires on the forklift were hot. Glad that none of them had blown out, I went around to the other side of the trailer, near the rear tires. All the brake drums were glowing a hot red. I started shaking so much I had to lie down in the tall grass. Then the tears came and I was shaking all over as I laid there for a long time staring into the calming blue Hawaiian skies.

The sound of a car stopping next to the truck caught my attention. I just lay there, too weak to move. I heard footsteps passing through the tall grass. Looking up, I saw a policeman. "Hey, you okay, are you all right?" Slowly he helped me sit up and I leaned back against the rear tires of the trailer. Wiping my eyes, the only thing I was able to say was "Wow what a ride." Thinking he might tell me I couldn't park my truck here, I heard him ask again, "Hey, you okay, that was some ride you just had."

Puzzled, I looked at him as he spoke. *"I was at the first light when I saw you come roaring through the intersection. I knew you were in trouble and I followed you down the hill. On that last steep stretch I clocked you at well over 120 mph. Ya, I lost my brakes in the second tunnel at the top of the Pali."*

His eyes got big. "What?" *Why didn't you go for the ramp?"*
"That's not where I wanted to die." After pausing I asked him, "Brah, do you surf?

What's the biggest wave you ever rode?"

He replied, *"I surfed in my younger days, the biggest wave was about 20 feet."*

I began to tell him of my experience. "This ride down the Pali reminded me of surfing my first big wave. It was around 1965, a holiday maybe Christmas or New Years, maybe it was Thanksgiving and the south shore was cranking up to about 20 feet. We were way outside of Magic Island trapped with monster sets pounding us continuously. I was so afraid I wanted to go back in, but the only way was to catch one of these monsters. I tried paddling for a couple waves trying to get some momentum, while at the same time hoping I would miss the wave because it was too big and scary.

Then when I wasn't ready, I found myself picking up speed and sliding down the face of a giant wave. Once I had the forward motion on the wave I was committed. The drop was steep. I had a chance to kick out, but I knew I would get clobbered. So I hung in there. The wave kept rising there was no backing out. The lip started to curl, white water pouring over as I got locked in. There was no way out except to ride this wave, stay focused, concentrate and hope for the best. The long wall on the right was ready to close out, I didn't think I would make that section and I had to do a long left turn to cut back. That was my only option, I was committed. There was no way off this mountain of a wave and I had to ride it out. I made the tube, beat that section as it broke behind me and hung in there knowing I still might not make it and possibly would get drilled."

He understood what I was trying to relate to him. I continued, "Brahdah, this wild ride down the mountain was just like being on a big wave with many obstacles coming at you. Hey, you don't think I planned this ride down the hill? It happened and I had to deal with it." I let him know it was a gamble, but I was ready to take the rig off the mountain if I came close to hitting somebody. I wasn't afraid to die.

He looked at me for a long time then responded, "Man, somebody was watching over you, 'cause you certainly lived up to your company name….Semi-Pro."

"Yeah, it's a long story, but I had to put my trust in faith. It was all up to God if I was going to live or die today. It was God and his Angels who brought my truck safely down the mountain today. Sometimes I live on the edge and take risks but today was a calculated risk and I had confidence I would survive. Today God was watching me and knew I was in trouble. He and my Angels answered my prayers. Thank you Lord."

If you live in the Enchanted Lakes area of Kailua, there are two homes on Alihi Street tiled with that load of "green" roofing tile. Man if those tiles could talk. I would say those two homes are truly blessed.

CHAPTER 19

The DC-6, work horse for the Air Force and cargo companies worldwide.

FINAL APPROACH

In my early twenties my life style in Southern California was exciting to say the least. I could never get enough of life in the fast lane. Always one for living on the edge, I constantly needed to fill my appetite for high-speed action, thrills and excitement. Being a typical young American male, I had a hunger for fast super stock motorcycles and hotrods, dune buggies, dirt bike racing, speedboats and downhill snow skiing. I was your basic all around sports nut. Then I discovered a new thing, another high.

One day while driving my big semi truck through the Mohave Dessert in California, I pulled over at some dive coffee shop in the middle of the dessert to grab a cold pop and I came across a poster hanging on a wall. This was a one-horse town with the local post office in this mom and pop store along with one gas pump and one diesel pump. It was called the Whistle Stop, probably named for the train that stops here twice a week as it went through this deserted stretch of land. The poster caught my eyes because it had a giant picture of Smokey the Bear wearing his Forest Ranger outfit and cap, except he was holding a lighted box of matches. The caption across the top of the poster said, "Burn Baby Burn." If you saw it, you would stop to check it out too because it seems that my hero was promoting forest fires. Something was wrong with this picture.

The poster was an advertisement for parachuting into

a forest fire and it was a way to recruit people to join up with this firefighting brigade. It had a map to their training facility, way out in the middle of nowhere, in the Mohave Dessert. I ripped the poster off the wall and walked back to my truck thinking hhmmm, maybe this is something I needed to do, parachute, skydive, drop into a hot spot and fight fires.

A week went by and I was trucking through the desert again so I made a beeline toward this area, way out in the boonies. I wanted to find out more about this forest fire thing and training to jump into a hot spot from an airplane. I was ready for a new challenge and thought this was an adventure I was lacking so I signed up and could not wait for the rush that comes with free falling.

Within a week, I had accomplished the basic requirements in ground school, five static line jumps and five free falls. A static line jump is when you exit the aircraft and a cable connected to the airplane opens your chute. In a free fall, you jump out and free fall, then pull the ripcord yourself and your chute is supposed to open. If it didn't then you had to figure out if you're having a partial malfunction or a major screw up, all while dropping at ninety miles an hour. We had to practice opening our reserve pack while at the same time trying not to get it tangled with the main shoot that was messed up.

We were flying in old twin engine Beach Crafts and a lot of times there was a shortage of qualified pilots to fly these old twin prop birds that we were jumping out of. So on occasion I would slide into the right seat for some multi-engine flight training. As time went on, I lost interest in the fire fighting thing and the excitement of jumping and I became overwhelmed with flying the aircraft. I actually got to fly into a fire zone when we were needed to do an assessment on a brush fire that was starting to get bigger. Hooked, I started

learning how to fly and I was going to make it my future.
NOW FAST FORWARD AHEAD ABOUT FIFTEEN YEARS

Back in Hawaii years later I hung up my interstate boots and I hooked up with a small, private air cargo carrier. The company had the contract to deliver the local daily newspapers to every island, and guess who was flying in the right seat? I managed to satisfy the pilot with my flying capabilities and after a few check flights, he had enough confidence in me to let me do all the takeoffs, flying and landings in his twin-engine Cessna aircraft.

Starting at 11 p.m. the newspapers were loaded into the Cessna in Honolulu, bound for Lihue, Kauai. From there we would fly back to Honolulu, and load up more papers for Maui, Molokai and Lanai. After that we'd return to Honolulu and load up newspapers for Hilo, Kamuela and Kona on the Big Island of Hawaii. I tell you what, seeing the islands from 3000 ft. is spectacular and I managed to get a lot of flight time.

In time, I got on with Aloha Cargo Transport, (ACT) a contract cargo outfit, as a load master flying freight to the neighbor islands on a big DC-6, four-engine prop aircraft. In the cockpits the pilot sits on the left side, called the first seat and the co-pilot sits on the right side, the second seat. The flight engineer is behind them, in the center where he operates and controls a whole bunch of stuff including the power in each of the four big prop engines. Directly behind the flight engineer is a jump seat for two people and this is where I sat. The pilot and co-pilot take turns flying the aircraft on each leg of any trip. Who ever is doing the flying has the "con," the control of the flight.

Flying as we all know can have many dangerous and sometimes fatal encounters. One night, we experienced two close calls. It was about 1 a.m. and a statewide storm was pounding Hawaii. We were flying a return trip from Hilo to Honolulu when we were zapped by lightning and our navigational aids and some other electronic equipment got knocked out instantly. This should have been a red flag to cool it because this storm was getting worse by the hour. We landed in Honolulu and switched aircrafts to a plane loaded with cargo for Lihue, Kauai.

On this leg of the flight over to Kauai, my friend Duffy King would have the "con" in the second seat. When the check list was done, we taxied out to the reef runway and ran up the engines for a while and did another check list before rolling down to the staging area for departure. The storm was pounding us, the cross wind was ripping, shaking our big aircraft as we sat there. Every so often the crackle of lighting and the boom of thunder would vibrate through the cockpit. I was a little spooked thinking maybe we should abort this flight and wait out this storm front. But these pilots are professionals and they knew their stuff. We took off and in no time made it up above the storm.

The flight over to Kauai was uneventful because we were high above the storm that was wreaking havoc on the islands below us. This trip takes about 25 minutes and local time was 3:45 in the morning. About 10 minutes out the pilot contacted ground control for current weather conditions and the wind direction. This information helped us to plan our approach to the airport so we know what runway to use. The person at ground control talking to us on the radio was with the Aloha Cargo Transport and not with the airport traffic control tower because those folks go home after the last commercial flight leaves Kauai at about 9:15 in the evening. In fact the whole airport is closed down by10 p.m. The scratchy voice on the radio responded with the barometric pressure, the wind speed and direction. He also reminded us about the heavy intermittent down pours and flooded conditions at the north end of the runway and assured us that there were no other aircraft on the ground.

This would be a routine landing and we may be on the ground for an hour. We were five minutes away from final approach into Lihue Airport and I was in the rear of the aircraft securing a pallet of cargo when that familiar Voice came to me, clear and sharp, "Strap in, Strap in now." I wasn't quite finished tying down this pallet so I worked until it was done correctly and wouldn't come loose again on landing. Then the Voice, now more persistent warned, "Strap in now, Strap in."

I made my way back to the cabin because I knew we would be on final approach at any second. Everything was smooth at our altitude above the clouds. The pilots started our descent down into the stormy night when suddenly we got ROCKED. I never made it to my seat directly behind the flight engineer. The force of the jolt pinned me against the electric panel on the left side of the cockpit. The stormy weather was so intense that the wipers could not handle the rains heavy force.

When entering Lihue Airport in normal trades, planes first line up with the harbor entrance staying to the right of a mountain peak, and then do a hard bank to the right to line up for the final approach to the runway. This was in the early eighties before the new runways were built. Visibility was so bad we couldn't see the mountain peak. "Cheesez," somebody uttered as we descended into the stormy night sky. Now we were under 500 feet, but where was that mountain? The rain was so intense it was as if a fire hose had been turned loose on us. The winds were howling. Flying on instruments with the harbor just below us, we saw a bright glow of lights that told us we were just above the Club Jetty. Now with a sharp bank to the right, at 450 feet and descending, wheels down and locked, flaps down 15 degrees, we are on final approach.

The runway for Lihue should be out there-somewhere. The aircraft began pitching drastically, almost 30 degrees. This is the scene everyone dreads if you're not used to flying. The plane is rolling to the opposite side, far off the level indicator. With zero visibility at 350 feet and dropping, the downpour was pounding us, definitely a nasty storm to attempt a landing. Suddenly out of nowhere, our aircraft is sucked down by a wind sheer, then a second later a heavy gust of wind hit us on the starboard side moving our aircraft well off to the left into another direction, away from the runway. Our alert warning systems was letting us know we were on a direct collision with the ground.

We were below 200 feet and visibility was still poor and we could make out something directly in front of us. The Lihue Airport's traffic control tower was dead ahead. With warning alarms and buzzers going off, the pilot is whispering, "Pull up! Pull up!" We were below 100 feet and the tower was closing in fast. The loud roar of our four props was evidence that the flight engineer turned up the power. If it wasn't effective in a few seconds, we were going down and into the tower. This situation was looking bad. I called my hot line connection and said a prayer asking for immediate help, when almost instantly, a feeling of calmness came over me, and the assurance that we would be okay.

Our aircraft made a desperate dive to the right, making a three-point landing, first on the right wing landing gear, then bouncing up and coming down on the nose landing gear, rolling left and touching down on the left landing gear. With another short bounce we finally touched down on all three landing gears at the same time, on the apron directly in front of the Lihue terminal and air traffic control tower. Now silence, we were down, we were safe, and we were lucky!

At the same time everyone whispered, "Thank God!" As the aircraft taxied down the runway, no one said a word. Then Duff quips, "Was anybody scared?" The pilot exclaims, "That was way too close!" As he calmed down, the flight engineer queried, "How did we get out of that?" Both pilots looked at each other trying to figure out who made the last second dive to the right. Then Duff asked, "How did that right wing hold up? We came down hard." I managed to speak, "Hey, it was a miracle. Thank God. This wasn't an average landing tonight but God and Duffy brought us down safely." This was my time to say a silent prayer of thanks because we were kept safe.

Two days later Duff and I were working on the same flight in Kona and we had some time to kill while the ground crew strapped down the cargo in the aircraft. Duff says, "So how bout that landing in Lihue, was that a trip or what?"

I told him, "Yeah man, that was almost our final trip, thanks for raising my blood pressure."

"No man that was a close call, it was a miracle we survived that one" Duff replied.

I said, "Hey Duff, I have confidence in you and your flying abilities, we got hit by a wind shear in a bad storm and you pulled us out."

It wasn't but a few months after that close call landing in Lihue, Kauai, when my plans of pursuing a flying career ended abruptly. I was surfing on a big wave day, outside at Hanalei Bay on Kauai when I was involved in a nasty surfing collision, seriously injuring my spine, and drowning. Found lifeless on the ocean floor, I was revived and ended up in

Wilcox Hospital partially paralyzed. That's another story and I don't know when I'm going there.

Years went by and Duff and I saw each other occassionally. One day while I was doing my thing as a sign painter on the movie sets, I saw Duff. We sat down and talked for a while. By now, he had stepped up to jet planes, flying for Hawaiian Air. It just so happened that today he was doing a check flight on a seaplane that was to be used in this movie.

I told him I was writing a book about miracles and he got really interested and wanted to find out more. He asked if I would write a story about our close call landing in Lihue years ago. I gave it some thought and said well, maybe. Duff offered to help me on all the technical terms for a DC-6, and describe everything that's happening when the DC-6 aircraft is on final approach. I thought wow, what a great idea, maybe I should do this story. He said he was heading over to Molokai for the weekend to do some hang gliding and when he returned then perhaps we could get together to write this story, and maybe call it "Final Approach." I said, "Shoots brah, I think you got a great idea so call me next week, and stay safe under those kites. Sea ya."

My Friend Duffy King never made it back to Honolulu to his friends and loved ones.

This story goes out to the memory of my friend, Captain Duffy King. An accomplished pilot, Duff flew with several local airlines here in Hawaii including Mid Pacific Air, DHL, and Hawaiian Air. Duff loved flying and had a passion and serious interest for hang gliding. It was this dangerous sport that took him from us while hang gliding on Molokai, at such a young age. He was a great friend to everyone who knew him.

Captain Duffy, Aloha.

ENDORSEMENTS

> *The steps of a good man are ordered by the Lord....*
> *For the Lord upholds him with his hand.*
> PSALMS 37:23-24 NKJV

Back in 1993, Kii told me about a book he was writing and let me read a typed manuscript. I was the first to read **Something Told Me** and encouraged him to provide it to others by having it published. People's lives would be strengthened when they see how the Lord has worked in his life.

It is evident to see that God, through the Holy Spirit, was working out his purposes in this man's life. He is God's man at the right place, at the right time. He will listen to that still small voice of the Holy Spirit within him and say, "Yes Lord, Here I am, No crisis is too great with faith in the Lord."

Kii has a gift, a holy anointing from God. I am happy to see this book finally becoming a reality. The stories are exciting and you will not want to put it down until it's finished. I wholeheartedly endorse this book.

Mr. Gale Wilson
Chaplain, (LTC) USA, RET
21 Years as a United States Army Chaplain

O Lord God, thank you for my friend Kiki.

His ability to hear the voice of God and obey the instructions given, enabled Kii to change many lives, including his own. Though, many are called by God, only a few hear His voice and have the opportunity to experience God in that arena. I believe that Kii experienced a supernatural "one on one" connection with God, as revealed in the stories that he has shared.

"Something Told Me," will encourage you to keep your ears open and listening...not to something, but to someone.

Aloha! Pastor Dick Jensen

About the Author

    Born with the gift of multiple intelligences, Wai Kiki is a talented individual, who for years has shuffled five professions on a weekly basis. Aside from being multi- professional and multi-talented, his platter is always full with other projects because his talents are so diverse in many areas.

 1) BOAT CAPTAIN. He has worked in the Maritime Industry for 15 years and holds a United States Coast Guard Captain license and is a licensed U.S. Merchant Marine. Currently he is the Senior Pilot Boat Captain with the Hawaii Harbor Pilots in Honolulu.

2) SIGN PAINTER. A professional artist for the past 37 years, he owns Signs and Stuff, fabricating all types of signs in wood and metal. He is one of a handful of sign painters left in Hawaii that specializes in the dying art of free-hand lettering on banners, big trucks, yachts, boats, aircrafts and also for the movie industry in Hawaii.

3) TRUCKER. For over 30 years he has been in the trucking industry as a big truck owner and operator. He owns Semi-Pro Trucking, a small fleet of semi trucks that service the maritime industry in Hawaii. He is a former interstate trucker who has traveled the USA from coast to coast and from Canada to Mexico.

4) MUSICIAN. He's had a serious passion for music all his life and is an accomplished musician who plays music on a regular basis. He has done studio sessions as a back up guitarist and has the sensitive talent of playing by ear while at the same time appreciates the melody and rhythm in any style including Latin, Country, Blue Grass and Hawaiian.

5) PUBLISHER. His latest project, writing this book, has been in the works for 13 years. Determined to self publish this book project, he started Wonder Horse Publications and presently he is in the studio to record the Audio CD version of Volume one. Volume two is already scheduled to be released by this spring along with a second Audio CD. Following this he already has orders to publish five other books.

About the Book

Edited By
Pat Lopes

Book Design and Production
Wai Kiki and Jackie Kahookele Burke

Layout/Graphics
Jackie Kahookele Burke

Cover Design [Front and back]
Wai Kiki

Art Work
Mark Brown

About the Cover

Original painting done by Mark Brown. The title is the author's inspiration for the commissioned painting, "First Light after the Hurricane."

Photo Credits

One Gutsy Move – Gaylord Wilcox, John Lind, Micheal Tongg, Jeffery Young, Wally Froiseth and Wai Kiki.

Ordering the book and information

www.wonderhorsepublishing.com
e-mail info@wonderhorsepublishing.com